Victoria's Dilemma

PATRICIA HUTH

Copyright O Patricia Huth 2023

Same Author Publishing 2023

ISBN 9798390106976

Patricia Huth asserts the moral right to be identified as the author of this work.

This book is sold subject to the condition that it shall not, by way of trade or otherwise, be lent, re-sold, hired out or otherwise circulated without the author's prior consent in any form of binding or cover other than that in which it is published and without a similar condition including this condition being imposed on the subsequent purchaser.

The Moving Finger writes; and having writ
Moves on: nor all thy Piety not wit
shall lure it back to cancel half a line
Nor all thy Tears wash out a word of it.

Omar Khayyam

For Tiffany, with love

My name is Victoria Scott. In 1963 I married Leo Scott, publisher, and had three children, Harriet, Tom and Sarah. In 1984 I left him and came to live in Wellchester, a cathedral town due south of Marlborough. This is my diary for 1985, recounting the events that made up my life in the first year of being re-singled, aged 42.

CHRISTMAS DAY
Tuesday 25th December, 1984

The much dreaded Christmas Day was just as black as I had expected. Matins at Wellchester Cathedral was overflowing with happy families. Singing "Once in Royal David's City" I thought of other Christmases with my children, and wept. On returning home I found the turkey still in the fridge instead of in the oven, so I had cod-in-parsley sauce out of a packet for Christmas lunch this year.

Spoke on the telephone to Harriet, Tom and Sarah who hoped I were having a happy Christmas. I said I wasn't, and as far as I was concerned Christmas was a washout and the sooner it was over the better. At five o'clock I opened a bottle of white wine (not Sancerre) and drank the entire contents by 5.22. For the rest of the festival, thankfully, I was oblivious.

I did have a word with JC before passing out. Why, I asked Him, did He not express the wish somewhere in the Good Book that His birthday should never, on any account, be celebrated? The distress caused by Christmas every year, particularly for divorced and single people, is infinite. The measure of sorrow only known to those without, for whatever reason, their own flesh and blood.

BOXING DAY
Wednesday 26th December

Boxing day or not with no wrapping paper to discard, no turkey to re-hash, and no family quarrels to umpire, the day felt as any other winter Wednesday. I listened to Old Thyme Music on the wireless. Someone called Ben was making awful jokes. Sarah rang to say she had fallen in love with a boy called Cosmo at a party. Could I remember anyone who lived in Kirtlington, she said, with a son called Cosmo since she wished to re-acquaint herself with him. Children are so odd not asking each other for their surnames. I told her I knew of no such person.

Felt sharp pains behind my eyes today and in my hands. At nearly 43 arthritis, middle-age and the menopause to look forward to in 1985. Decided to renew my typing skills at the local C.F.E. although I know I am not suited, temperamentally, to secretarial work.

I read some Mrs. Gaskell before going to bed. I expect she spent her Christmases and Boxing Days with her family.

Thursday 27th December

Diana Cassington-Mackenzie rang to say she was lunching in Wellchester and would drop in to see me afterwards. She brought various offerings in a basket, namely butter, home-made cranberry sauce, marmalade and two packets of digestive biscuits. It struck me that her nanny, who had lived in a similar Victorian house to mine, and I, were somewhat confused in her mind. Perhaps she thought terrace dwellers needed sustenance as presents, not scented soap and bitter mints. I ate nine digestive biscuits when she left which will made me even fatter. I keep wondering why I gave up smoking. I enjoyed smoking when I smoked. The racy smell of Gauloise cigarettes, and the curious sensual excitement of lighting up and puffing smoke all over the place was a delight I still greatly miss.

Telephoned Father's Old People's home, Blueberry Rise. Matron said that most of the "old folk" had had a great Christmas. Father was not one of them however. He was troubled with his teeth and wanted to know nothing of the turkey and its trimmings. Or the Christmas pudding. When mother was alive and made the pudding she put dangerous pieces in it, he told Matron, and her family, as a consequence, all became ill. At supper I listened to the Archers. Tony and Pat Archer are now organic farmers; an interesting piece of progress.

Incidentally the information that my father gave the matron regarding dangerous pieces in the Christmas pudding was not true.

Friday 28th December

Had the feeling that I was the only person left on earth. The streets were deserted and the silence was infinite. Stayed in bed all morning and read some William Trevor short stories. His wit is ever delightful and makes me laugh out loud. Harriet and Tom think his work is "mega boring." I answered an advertisement I saw in Private Eye's Christmas edition. The advertisement said: "English teacher now back in England would like to meet intelligent woman for walks, and talks and who knows .... " I replied that walks and talks sounded promising, but I wasn't certain about the who knows bit. My letter caught the 6 o'clock post.

Tom rang to say that he and friends were going to Bristol for the weekend therefore he would not be coming here as arranged. What shall I do with all the food I have bought? Children are so bloody inconsiderate.

A man on the wireless gave a talk on "knowing yourself." I have a theory that knowing yourself is impossible. I suspect we have many different consciousnesses which surface at different times, changing our personalities and thus our behavior. Otherwise why are neighbours constantly astonished that the nice man-next-door who fed their cat whilst they were on holiday murdered his mother with a meat hatchet?

I read late but reading small print is more difficult than it was last year. I suppose I will need glasses soon.

Saturday 29th December

Shops open again with crackers at half price. For next Christmas perhaps? Saw Steve McQueen at the Regal. It is the fourth time I have seen this film. Steve McQueen is the only macho man I have even glanced at and imagined kissing. In real life I expect he was terribly boring and never spoke or read a book, least of all 19th century novels.

I must remember to get locks on the windows and a bolt for the door on Monday. Living alone is frightening, and all noises sound menacing before the dawn breaks. JC promised to be always with me and I believe Him but I think locks are essential for added security and true tranquility. I am sure He understands this piece of reasoning.

Sunday 30th December

Went to lunch with Gillian and Simon Hayes in Dorset. They produced a single man for me to "make up numbers." His name is Henry Rose and he had been forced out of familiar and comfortable solitude. He was small of stature and said little. That type of Englishman, I felt, who sexually hasn't even made up his mind exactly what he is. Single men, d'un certain age, are almost impossible to find. Those found are invariably homosexual or live with their mothers. Either way their interest in divorced middle-aged women is minimal.

Driving home alone I felt ineluctably that single people are still an oddity and that couples are still the norm. The questions I ask myself now are: Whether to find another mate for 1985? Is it possible to fall in love again at 42, or am I too old, too worn out, too cynical, too deja-vu, or am I too excited by this newly acquired freedom to want to anyway? I don't know yet. I shall have to wait and see.

I rang Blueberry Rise. Father, said Matron, was developing a passion for a female patient. Love then, it seems, is not, like most other things, exclusively for the young.

As milk is, I know, fattening, I made a bedtime chocolate drink with hot water, and it was disgusting.

Monday 31st December

Apparently snow fell all over England during the night. My garden was completely covered with it. The birds were silent, shocked perhaps by its sudden arrival. I stuffed two nets of peanuts and hung them on the wall.

Liz came to lunch. Gus, she said, who was given a motor bike for Christmas, had fallen off it on Boxing Day and now couldn't walk properly. Liz said he was driving her mad, sitting in his room all day playing Heavy Metal music and sneaking down to the fridge in the night to take out cans of beer - beer that she was keeping for Rodney. This surprised me because I was convinced Rodney did not drink beer, and that it was Liz herself who liked a drop or two.

Liz said she wished the Christmas break was over and that she was back at work, peacefully, in the library. Everyone, I suspect, wishes that the Christmas festivities only lasted two days, instead of the now seemingly compulsive two weeks. By the end of them, most families have quarrelled so violently and viciously that it could take until next Christmas to patch up the squabbles when, without doubt, they would start all over again.

I made a coal fire and warming myself by it, I ate a cheese omelette and listened to Beethoven's Fifth Symphony. At midnight I was asleep and the New Year came in without my knowledge, whilst people all over England were probably singing Auld Lang Syne or being sick, or both.

On retiring I spoke to JC about His timetable for 1985. Less poverty, less war, less violence and much less stupidity on the parts of the World Leaders, would be popular with everyone I thought, and advised Him accordingly.

Tuesday 1st January

Another non-day with no shops open, no post and no newspapers. The end of the world will probably feel like this.

Matron at Blueberry Rise said father had sneaked two glasses of sherry at the New year's party and, as a consequence, was having trouble with his digestion and his temper. I am glad mother is dead, she hated father in a temper.

This afternoon I cut up some curtains to use for my patchwork, and started sewing a tablecloth. I listened to a radio play set in the United States. The dialogue was quite incomprehensible with people talking about "short term adaptive advantages" and "moderate depressive symptomatology" and other similar rubbish. Perhaps Americans, in time, will take over not only our heritage, but also our native tongue.

I missed my children today. It was my first Christmas alone and divorced and I felt nostalgic and sorry for myself. I went to bed and asked JC to send the consolation that is expected from Him for middle-aged women when nothing else seems possible or probable.

Wednesday 2nd January

Post and papers came today. Is normality returning, I wonder? Had a postcard from one Guy Bell, a fellow student I met, apparently, at a Philosophy Summer School last year in Warwick. Would I like to have a drink with him when he came to Wellchester next week? it said. I can't remember what he looks like - but I do remember he was a psychologist. Perhaps I will go if he rings. But since people's words are NOT currently their bonds, I have little expectation that he will do so.

The snow has melted and the garden looks gloomy and bleak. Last year's sweet pea shoots that I meant to take out in October are trailing miserably to the ground.

Harriet, Tom and Sarah are coming at the weekend so I made marmalade. After lunch I resuscitated my old typewriter and tried typing a bit. My memory did not serve me wrong - my typing is as appalling as I do not think those of nervous disposition are suited to typing.

Leo rang to say he had got married again. He had known the woman for years, he said, and she also lived in Brighton. I wished him all the luck in the world and said I thought anyone would make a better wife than I had. Later I felt a strange jealousy for someone unknown, who is taking her place in life beside a man I thought I no longer cared for and had abandoned. My emotions are completely incomprehensible to me - try as I might I cannot get them to follow the sensible and philosophical path of reason.

The marmalade had set so I put it into large glass jars and left it on the kitchen table when I went up to bed. Before turning out the light I read Philip Larkin's poem that starts: "They fuck you up, your mum and dad. They may not mean to but they do". Yes Philip Larkin, they do, they do.

Philip Larkin, for all his bicycle clips, "flasher mac", dislike of London and foreigners, and worse, lack of a sociology degree, knew life's absolute truths.

Thursday 3rd January

Father Murphy from Blackfriars visited today. I was washing my hair when he called and I offered him tea in the kitchen. Then I dripped all over him and the tablecloth. He seemed obsessed with Joan of Arc and being celibate. Did I know, he said, or could I possibly understand the agonies he had to bear as a celibate priest? I said rather meanly that it had been his choice. No one forces men into priesthood as far as I know. He left in a sulk saying I was a hard woman, and anyway, most of the Irish housewives who came to his confessional were in love with him. (So there?) I suppose people who are celibate for whatsoever reason, talk and think more about sex than those who get their fair portion. I must take heed.

Sarah rang to say she, Tom and Harriet would arrive by train tomorrow. Daddy had married again, she said, to a lovely woman called Grace. The only Grace I ever knew committed suicide by jumping into the sea, in winter, from the cliffs of Dover. I hope that Leo's Grace won't do the same thing, although once married to him, she might feel tempted.

Blueberry Rise rang to say father had broken his false teeth and could I do something about it. What, I wonder? Perhaps I should buy some Evo-stik and glue them together as I did with the children's toys years ago.

Friday 4th January

Saw a job advertised in the Wellchester Echo for the position of assistant in a flower shop. I am going to see the manageress on Monday. Since my knowledge of flowers is almost nonexistent and I find it difficult to tell a chrysanthemum from a cyclamen, I bought a paperback on house plants and their care. It is interesting to note how each plant wishes to be treated as an individual, with special requirements for feeding, watering and sunlight. This information supports my opinion that man and nature are part of an organic whole. The moral courage to express one's individuality seems to me one of the few principles in life worth fighting for.

Harriet, Tom and Sarah arrived together after tea. I was very pleased to see them. Sarah had tied her hair up in a pony-tail with a bright scarf she had been given for

Christmas, and looked much older than 16. After supper we played Trivial Pursuit and Tom won, which pleased me since I know men like winning. I, myself, think it is a stupid game - as if anyone cares what a notaphily collects, or who won the Cup Final in 1967. For my part, I don't give a damn whether I win or lose Trivial Pursuit, or any other game, for that matter.

Saturday 5th January

   I dragged the groaning children to a Craft Fair in Marlborough. I think Craft Fairs are lovely - English in the best tradition - but the children think they are incredibly boring, twee, and embarrassing to be seen at. I left them grumbling, at the beer tent, to look around on my own, and I suppose it is true to say "once you have seen one ... " but I did buy 1/2 lb of home-made vanilla fudge. It was delicious and I ate it all myself. Sarah and Harriet quarrelled most of the day children are so tedious when they quarrel.
   We went to a cheap Italian restaurant for dinner where the Italian waiters chatted up the girls, which cheered them up. Since the food itself was uneatable and the Italian wine undrinkable, I was grateful. If Englishmen understood even a fraction about paying compliments to women their life would improve no end.
   Tonight I read the 23rd Psalm. Different age groups get different cheer from different things, I thought as I put out the light.

Sunday 6th January

Went to Matins at Wellchester Cathedral. The sermon was absolute drivel. The vicar said Christmas feelings of good will towards men should last more than just Christmas week. He delivered this message as if it was a totally new revelation. I stopped listening and looked about. There were rows and rows of stone saints over the altar, which led me to wonder what you had to do to qualify. All the people I know who are thought of as "saints" are extremely tiresome.

After lunch we went down to the canal ostensibly to enjoy a walk. This we were unable to do since Sarah insisted on taking Mr. Patel's Pyrenean Mountain dog, Bucket, with us (Mr. Patel of No. 13). Bucket ran away immediately he was set free. For the rest of the afternoon we tried to recapture him. It took until four o'clock, when it was quite dark and very cold. Sarah was not popular. She is going to buy a rabbit to take with her to the 6th form college in Marlborough which she starts next week.

At 7.02 I put the children on a train to Brighton. Grace, no doubt, will give them a delicious supper. Step-parents must, I imagine, find feeding their step-children something of a nuisance.

In the bath I listened to a woman folk singer and judged her performance quite good. But not as good as Joan Baez. I do miss the PASSION of Joan Baez's songs. Where are all the freedom fighters of today? Watching the television, I suppose.

Monday 7th January

I inspected my pot plants this morning and found most of them had died over Christmas. I had starved them of water and, unlike the overindulgence of humans at this time of year, undernourished, my plants had simply wilted to death. Although, I dare say, many people felt like wilting to death over the holiday and dying for them would probably have been a welcome release.

Had an interview with Mrs. Pratt, the manageress at Rose's Flower Shop. I think I made up in charm what I lacked in knowledge, but there are quite a few things against me even now, as I know nothing of shop work and even less about flowers. I told Mrs. Pratt untruthfully, as Mr. Toad told the washerwoman about his love of washing, that one thing in the world that I had always wanted to do was to work in a flower shop. She appeared impressed, and said she would let me know her decision at the end of the week after interviewing other applicants.

Liz rang this evening to say that thankfully she was back working at the library. Our children are impossible, she said. Yesterday, when she was cleaning Gus's bedroom she had found pornographic magazines and bits of old, uneaten paste sandwiches under his bed. An awful shock, she said, but better than finding them under Rodney's side of the marital bed - the magazines, not the sandwiches. I didn't say so to Liz but I shouldn't think that Rodney would appreciate in the least the nature of pornographic text and pictures. I suspect Rodney's sexual initiation, if any, took place in the late 50s, and he doesn't look the man to me to learn new tricks.

I picked up father's false teeth from Blueberry Rise and wrapped them in a handkerchief. False teeth look quite menacing when they are not in a mouth.

Tuesday 8th January

A postcard from Klosters arrived from Diana Cassington-Mackenzie. She and all her family and several other friends are apparently "whooping it up" on a jolly skiing holiday. Remembering my own experiences skiing, even the thought of it depresses me. I could visualize all forms of humanity, in very close proximity, queuing, queue barging, screaming, laughing, shouting, freezing, swearing, crying, boiling, fighting and fainting. If I had a straight choice today between skiing holiday in St Moritz or a Butlins holiday in Scunthorpe, I would choose Butlins with no prevarication.

Sarah started working for her A-levels at the Plato 6th Form College, a part of Marlborough School now taking girls. She rang to say she had settled in and that the other girls seemed nice. She would suspend the purchase of the rabbit until later in the term she said.

I left father's teeth with the dentist, who said that they would take a week to mend. Can gums chew solids I wonder, or what will he eat next week?

A.N. Wilson wrote an excellent article in the Spectator, explaining the Trinity, which I read in bed. I am very relieved that I now understand it, at least in part, since this vital issue in Christianity had always eluded me. It is difficult to work out, on your own, how someone can be three people at the same time.

Wednesday 9th January

I started a "sensational" new diet. It seems remarkably like others I have tried. Which ones haven't I tried? I have dieted for twenty years and feel there is nothing "new" or "exciting" or "sensational" about any of them, or ever will be. Nor do I imagine that I shall have any more success on this one than I have on the numerous others attempted. "Eat less, exercise more" is the best advice for those of us who wish to make ourselves slimmer, but strangely, knowing this to be so, we seem incapable of putting it to good effect.

Guy Bell telephoned at 4.47pm. He was staying at the Wellchester Arms and asked me for a drink tomorrow night, which I accepted. Hope does, in spite of evidence to the contrary, still spring eternal in my breast. (It is when hope stops springing that overdoses get taken, I suspect.)

I ironed my one black skirt in preparation for the occasion and thought of married days when I had so many choices. But choice makes life so complicated; the less I have, the better I manage. The black skirt is my only skirt so no time was wasted deciding "what to wear." With the time saved I read a piece in the newspaper about the Royal Family's financial troubles. It was of course, very distressing.

Made an appointment with the optician.

Thursday 10th January

Grapefruit, black coffee and a thin slice of unbuttered whole meal bread was the recommended breakfast allowance for today. However by 10.15 I felt hungry and ate two digestive biscuits.

After much deliberation I bought window and door locks. Knowing my own limitations with keys and their constant absence when needed, decided against buying a front door lock that needed unlocking inside in order for me to get outside, in case of fire in the night or somesuch. By the time I had found the key the house would have burned down, with me in it. Or the rapist would have raped me. So I bought large bolts and chains which the firm's "man" secured this afternoon. In future, although the house could be said to resemble Fort Knox, I will sleep more peacefully.

I met Guy Bell in the Wellchester Arms Lounge Bar. I recognized his clothes before I remembered his face since he distinctly resembles a man I saw in the film "Seven Brides for Seven Brothers," who sang, with others, "Bless Your Beautiful Hide" whilst cutting down stretches of forest somewhere in America. A kind of intellectual-Guardian-reading, pipe-smoking lumberjack in tartan shirt, jeans, corduroy jacket and brown lace-up boots.

We talked about our recollections of the Philosophy Summer School as one does with people met on holiday or encountered in other irregular meeting places, and after we had gone through that, silence fell. As a middle-aged and middle-class woman, trained to question, I asked him about himself. This is a consistently successful technique with men, and Guy, no exception, was happy to talk about himself. He is a psychologist, working in Bristol, was married for nine years and is now divorced. He lives alone in a cottage near Bath with his dog. The dog is called Dog.

I like him but he is not in the least bit merry, and laughs little. He seems a trifle intense about politics and his views, I feel, coincide with those Witten in The New Statesman. I know of course, that Mrs. Thatcher penalizes academics and is something of a philistine, but who else is there to govern us, I ask myself (I asked him the same question), since the S.D.P. are in such disarray? Guy said Tony Benn would do a good job which I thought was rubbish, and said so. A political argument was terminated only when he had to leave to catch the 8.10 back to Bristol. He said, as parted, he would telephone we next me when in Wellchester and perhaps we could dine together? I agreed, quite enthusiastically, that that might be enjoyable.

Is Guy Bell sexually attractive I asked myself on retiring to bed. In actual fact I asked myself the same question on the bus home. But the answer I gave myself, on both occasions, was not conclusive. He is not the man dreams are made of, certainly. He is matter-of-fact, precise and not, I suspect, in the least romantic, a quality I wish for in a suitor. But still...

Sexual desire, for me, I thought, has never been immediate - it requires nurturing at a slow and quiet pace, in order to develop. Ineluctably, I now know I need someone whom I can trust and love and who, in turn, will trust and love me before desire and intimacy arise. Without these two essential ingredients sex would mean less than nothing, and even if my body did not suffer unduly, my spirit undoubtedly would. Sex for myself, I have decided, can only be contemplated where love is. Perhaps, therefore, I shall be a long time celibate, and only hope it doesn't affect me as adversely as modern thinkers would have us believe.

 I ate a Mars Bar before going to sleep, which was not specified on the diet.

Friday 11th January

Heard Lady Someone-or-Other on the radio at breakfast advising the nation to talk to their house plants. They would, as a result she said, flourish and grow in a "truly amazing way." Should I, I ask myself, address the three iceberg roses I planted just before Christmas in my garden - which appear to be dying - and hope for the same effect? The British aristocracy, as a dying species, might be best remembered in years to come for the "truly amazing" nonsense they talk.

 Mrs. Pratt telephoned to offer me morning employment in her shop, starting, on Monday. Congratulations Victoria, I thought, and this evening I rang to tell Liz the news. She seemed somewhat unenthusiastic and said she knew of people who had serious breathing problems working indoors all day among foliage and flowers. Asthma could be contracted in that sort of employment, she said. In fact she wanted to tell me about Gus. She had, she said, in no uncertain manner, chastised him about the paste sandwiches and pornographic magazines left under the bed. Apparently he told her to "piss off," and then he left the house slamming the front door. And, worse, he has dyed his hair pink. Rodney would have to be told of his impertinence and punish him when he got home. I felt Rodney would have no more success in meting out punishments than he would in acquiring new sexual techniques, but I agreed with Liz, untruthfully, that telling Rodney would be expedient.

"JC," I said, putting out the light, "I have found it is NOT always right to tell the complete truth; people's feelings have to be considered. Therefore, for the untruths I uttered today I will need no forgiveness since, in my opinion, no sin was committed."

Saturday 12th January

Had an answer from the advertisement in Private Eye, from one Peter Mallet. He is divorced, he wrote, and wished to re-marry. Do people, I wonder, reduce their ages by a year or two when advertising themselves or answering advertisements? Truths not being respected, or even expected these days, makes me think that Peter Mallet was probably not 39. He informed me, in the letter, that he had been out East for many years teaching English to Arabs. He didn't say whether it was English Language he taught or English Literature, but I think it must have been the latter since I don't suppose Arab children would appreciate the niceties of Jane Austen's temperate world, or even Dicken's, in spite of a certain degree of violence in Great Expectations. He lives outside Nottingham, I note, but "had a car and would travel." The letter didn't "touch a cord" or make "my heart sing" but nevertheless I shall arrange a meeting.

In addition to this letter, I had a p.c. from the dentist advising me that father's teeth were ready for collection. I must note a clean handkerchief will have to be found in which to wrap them. Apparently Father has been in decline this week and refuses to get out of bed until his teeth are returned to him and his mouth.

Rodney Ely came round uninvited, to mend the Hoover. Liz had sent him, he said. Liz likes him out of the house on Saturday mornings but I do wish she wouldn't send him here. I know he is a Warden in the Cathedral but he definitely has a creepy way of looking at me, and catching sight of my black bra in the washing left on the kitchen table he said, with a silly laugh, did I mind him observing that it looked like an ample cup. "Rodney," I said in a cold voice, "any thoughts you may have about cup sizes, big or small, keep to yourself." Diana Cassington-Mackenzie is, I know, on the lookout for a new lover. Perhaps I ought to introduce her to Rodney who, I suspect, is searching for something more exciting that Liz's embraces with the cocoa. Perhaps Diana could get him interested in her cups, or whatever, it is that needs attention. Rodney mended the Hoover, but it only worked for a moment or two, then smoke puffed out, blowing all the week's dust everywhere. Dying, apparently, it gave a short moan (like the Belle Dame sans Merci) and refused to move again. I shall probably have to buy a new one now. In truth, the more I see of other people's husbands, the less I want a new one of my own.

Surveying the iceberg roses during tea I noticed that they had derived no benefit whatsoever from a quick word I had with them this morning. They were, it seems, still dead.

Sunday 13th January

The text for the sermon at the cathedral this week was an old one, namely Matthew 22. v. 39, "Love Thy Neighbour as Thyself." The Bishop of Winchester gave a good sermon, but I think if everyone accepted the truth that human beings are not disposed to like one another, fewer people would be surprised and disappointed at their lack of success in changing this fact.

Matron at Blueberry Rise said father was now on strike and was refusing to co-operate with anyone, in any way, until the return of his teeth. I can pick them up tomorrow and shall hire a car to take them back to him on Tuesday evening. I wonder whether I will be as difficult as he when I am 76.

I tried to read the Sunday newspaper, which was full of scandal about lesser Royalty's proclivities for cross-dressing and general corruption, but unfortunately I could not see the small print. Reading glasses are now not a choice but an essential.

I gave up the diet altogether today. It is absurd to expect anyone to survive more than a day or two on black coffee and fruit and vegetables (preferably raw). I might have managed if it were compulsory to smoke 25 cigarettes between dawn and dusk, in addition to the diet, but since no mention was made of tobacco consumption, I abandoned it. I ate instead two jam Swiss rolls and a quarter of Rose's milk chocolates. That I felt much better goes without saying.

    I asked JC for a modicum of help tomorrow as I start work for Mrs. Pratt. I know He is busy at the moment sorting out the Far East and the crisis in the Sudan, but we all feel our own needs are unique and I am no exception to the rule.

Monday 14th January

    Knowing my inability to hurry I got up at 6.30 a.m., but, inevitably, I could not decide on suitable attire for a florist's assistant. All the clothes I possess ended up on the floor whilst time was running out. Finally I wore my navy skirt and white cotton shirt. A little nervous I thought fortification was needed before my first working day and I cooked eggs, bacon and sausages for breakfast. They were delectable. God knows why it has become fashionable in England during the latter part of this century, to eat breakfast in such a meagre way. Our ancestors could not have won wars and conquered India single-handed, as it were, on black coffee and muesli.

    In the event, I arrived at the shop ten minutes early. Mrs. Pratt, whose conversation is conducted almost entirely in cliches said, "new broom sweeps clean" as I greeted her. Perhaps conversation will be solely conducted in cliches in years to come to save ourselves the bother of having to think originally at all. I hope I am dead by then.

I sold an old lady a pot of hyacinths. She took twenty minutes deciding whether her niece would like the pink or the blue. Her niece's sitting-room was of a pale lemon she said and chose the pink. For my part, I thought this was an unwise choice but remembering my new principles of not absolute truth-telling, I said nothing.

Mrs. Pratt, I reflected, as I took the bus home, was a garrulous and vulgar woman, a gossip with a particular and voracious interest in the Royal Family. Did I think Princess Diana was satisfied sexually by Prince Charles? she had asked. She, herself, thought Princess Diana was not and prophesied that trouble would ensue. I said I had no thoughts whatsoever on the matter and indeed that it was of no interest to me, either way. But perhaps I am a bit of a prig.

Working in a shop will not be easy, I feel, but it is a job and I, with minimal maintenance and a mortgage to pay, will have to work where I can, whenever I can, in whatever capacity.

Tuesday 15th January

Had another p.c. from Diana Cassington-Mackenzie. She is now in Davos where, apparently, it is raining. However, with a choice of five cinemas open all day and discos, nightclubs and casinos open nearly all night, her skiing holiday cannot be as bad as my sun-holiday at Brancester beach last year when rain poured down every single day. I was given to understand that there was an amusement arcade in Hustanton but I, myself, did not try it. There were, indubitably, no casinos or discos.

Mrs. Pratt said that she thought the younger generation were unruly and obnoxious because they were on too many health foods. "My diet" she said, "which suits me admirably, has always been traditional English fare - like Yorkshire pudding, bread, potatoes, butter, beef, and Cadbury's chocolates." I didn't comment on this statement, since Mrs. Pratt, at a guess weighs about 14 stone.

I picked up Father's teeth from the dentist but forgot the clean handkerchief. I put them instead in a pre-paid envelope I had in my handbag which I should have used to send off an over-due cheque to the Gas Board. I hired a car and drove to Bath which looked beautiful, as usual, but Father spoiled my pleasure by his singular behavior. He refused to speak to me, but told Matron that the mended teeth were not fitting as they should. He then took them out and placed them in his left slipper. I left Matron to argue with him since I felt it was his perverse behavior that was at fault and NOT an error on the part of the dentist. I am glad that mother is now peacefully hors-de-combat. God knows she has earned the rest after forty odd years married to father.

I wrote a letter to Peter Mallet suggesting a meeting. I wish there was a casino in Wellchester to direct him to but since there is not I told him of The Crown Hotel in the High Street. Would the lounge bar at 7 O'clock on January 23rd be convenient, I wrote and enquired.

Two of the plants I bought last week have now died. That Mrs. Pratt never calls here will be, henceforth, included in my prayers.

Wednesday 16th January

I met Liz for lunch in the Health Food shop. "You are looking peaky," she said immediately she saw me. "It must be the result of working in a flower shop. There is, of course, less oxygen for your blood stream to absorb, surrounded by plants all day." Liz, I think, made up this piece of information since, to my certain knowledge, she knows nothing about oxygen or flower shops. I asked her about Rodney and she said (a) that he had spoken to Gus about his impertinence but that little improvement in his behaviour could be detected as a result and b) that he was a touch sulky on his return from mending my Hoover on Saturday morning. He had muttered something about feminist women who were the new plague of nations. Did I know exactly, she said, to what he was referring? I said I had no idea whatsoever.

Thursday 17th January

At 7.45 a.m. Sarah rang to say she and two friends would be coming into Wellchester on Sunday. They would come here for lunch she said, but could I note that they were all dieting. I have noted this fact and will, in consequence, only buy tomatoes, lettuce, and slices of York ham in Tesco's tomorrow. I expect they will only drink black coffee even though it is so disgusting.

Mrs. Pratt said she would train me to arrange wedding bouquets next week. This is quite an excitement to look forward to - working in the flower shop has not been, up to date, an invigorating experience. Perhaps St Valentine's Day will prove more entertaining with the sale of single red roses as Messengers of Love. But is the British male capable of Romance I ask myself.

At tea Father Murphy called. He was collecting jumble for a Bring-and-Buy morning in aid of Catholic Missions overseas. Over a cup of tea I thought it incumbent on me to state that: too many people worried themselves about unsatisfactory conditions abroad, while here in Britain there were still people suffering appalling deprivations. Nobody, I said, had Bring-and-Buy mornings for them. Father Murphy appeared to be not in the least interested at these observations. He told me instead about a young Irish girl in his parish who had become pregnant as a result of sexual intercourse with her math's teacher. Father Murphy had, of course, comforted her and told her that the Lord would provide. "I don't know why you told her that untruth Father Murphy," I said; "it won't be so much the Lord providing as the taxpayers." "God forgive you," said Father Murphy, "a stone lodges where your heart should be."

I rather like the image Father Murphy has of me as an aggressive feminist. I wish I had been one when I was married to Leo instead of a wet blanket, and I don't think I have changed much since. However, I do enjoy the performance I give to Father Murphy. It gives me a hitherto unknown feeling of power. I shall ask him to call here on a regular basis in order to practice my new assertive role. We could have time-wasting theological arguments based on his

Biblical studies and my intuition. And, one day, when I am feeling in a good mood, I might commiserate with him about his celibate state of being. If only Father Murphy knew the truth about the fantasy of life being so much superior to the reality. But I fear he never will. On leaving he said, "Visits to this house, Missus, will be constant. If for no other reason, I can save your soul." I do think Roman Catholics have got a nerve. My soul, I could have informed Father Murphy, is already in good hands.

Friday 18th January

    Mrs. Pratt said she had been up all night with indigestion. She thought the culprit was a piece of pre-cooked chicken she had bought in Tesco's, but I think - after she told me the menu - it was the amount of greasy chips that accompanied it, followed by a rich chocolate pudding. I did not, of course, divulge these thoughts to Mrs. Pratt.
    This afternoon I went to John Cassels, Opticians, in the High Street. It was very depressing. Mr. Hunt, the optician, kept repeating things like, "at your age, in middle age, after a certain age," and so on, with what appeared to be a certain amount of relish. Mr. Hunt, I would judge, was in fact not much younger than I am. He said, in essence, that after 40 the short-sighted could become less so, but that almost everyone started needing reading glasses at this stage of life. Oh vanity, vanity, despot of my life. Isn't it bad enough, dear Lord, to watch grey strands creeping through my hair, to feel my belt growing tighter as the days pass, and to be

stiff in the joints each morning without the inevitability of spectacles?

As I walked home, I thought that I would have to, in future, in order to attract men a) develop my cooking skills and b) possess intimate knowledge of the sex lives of the famous and fortunate. But where I should find these interesting pieces of information is difficult to imagine, since the famous and fortunate are not conspicuous in Maplewood Road, Wellchester.

I shall buy a cookery book I saw recommended in a copy of Good Housekeeping I read one Saturday morning in the dentist's waiting room. The magazine was, of course, four years out of date but since the book itself, apparently, sold over a million copies, I expect I shall be able to buy one, somewhere.

Saturday 19th January

Sarah and her two new friends, Rosemary and Louise, came for lunch. The tomato and lettuce salad I had prepared with honey ham was eaten up in no time. But they still seemed hungry. I found some cheese and a packet of digestive biscuits which they demolished quickly, almost without speaking. Nothing was said of their diets - perhaps they had since Thursday, abandoned the idea of dieting. They discussed, at lunch, the potential "talent" at Marlborough, or lack of it, either in the town or at the College. They had, they said, seen nothing whatsoever to attract their attention, let alone "go out with" or even join in a pub for a drink. Wellchester, that afternoon they hoped, would prove more fruitful. They left me with the washing up in order to maximize their searching hours.

Where were the days, I mused, as I washed up, of cocktail parties, dinners at the Savoy Hotel, or the Ritz, dancing at the 400 Nightclub, or of romantic music? Or was it, I wonder, just my children and their friends whose social life seemed to take place in Public Houses, or gathered on pavements, or squashed into bedsits overflowing with dirty clothes and full ashtrays?

Sunday 20th January

The heating system in the cathedral had broken down today. An icy wind blowing from the southwest penetrated every coming of the building making the Dean's sermon on the heat of hell fire seem inappropriate. Anyway quite some number of the congregation left before he spoke, in order no doubt to rush home and regenerate a little heat into their bodies while they were still able to move. The fur coat I wore, a purchase from Oxfam, kept me warm enough although my hands were too cold to turn the pages of the hymnbook. As I know the words of "Breathe of me, Breath of Life" (apposite under the circumstances) in the event it didn't matter. Sarah, Rosemary and Louise were still in bed at 1.45 p.m. When they did appear at tea time there was little said of the previous afternoon's or evening's activities. I assume therefore they did not find anything appropriate in the way of men in Wellchester's five pubs and two tearooms. They went back to Marlborough after eating everything edible I had in the house. What diet are they on I wonder.

Tonight, in bed, I started reading Proust's Remembrance of Things Past. I quite see that understanding Proust is an intellectual achievement and I am therefore determined to read all 1,500 or so pages of it. However, the first thirty-two pages I have read, proved very dull. If the next 1,468 pages are as uninteresting as these the project will be something of a struggle.

Monday 21st January

Had a letter from Peter Mallet and a p.c. from Diana Cassington-Mackenzie. Diana's postcard informs me that she is back from her dreadful (?) holiday and Peter Mallet will, he says, meet me at The Crown Hotel on Wednesday evening. The letter was written with a biro which does not bode well for an intimate relationship. I hate biros.

In my hurry to leave on Friday I had forgotten to water Mrs. Pratt's favourite plant, a red begonia, and it looked distinctly seedy this morning. In fact it was dead. Mrs. Pratt, when she discovered this misdemeanour on my part, was justly angry. "More haste, less speed," she muttered and said little else for the rest of the morning. Somehow the silence of Mrs. Pratt is worse than the speech.

Tom rang from Brighton and said Leo and Grace were going to Paris to buy some pictures, and that in consequence, he would come here for the weekend that they were away. Tom is so domestically lazy that the mere idea of cooking for himself, or worse, washing up, fill him with such dread that he would do anything to avoid such disaster. I will, of course, and do, wash up for Tom since I have always been too feeble to insist on his help. This has been a great mistake and his future wife will not thank me for so doing.

Father Murphy will not believe this weakness I have for indulging my son. But I think that all mothers of sons do, to some extent, love them not only unconditionally, but in a vaguely (or not so vague if the Greek myths are to be believed) sexual way. I have no way of knowing however whether this assumption is true or false; it is merely something I have always thought to be so. Why, I wonder frequently, is love so intangible. Everyone, it seems, wants love - to receive it and in turn to give it. And yet, although this would appear to be an apparently simple notion, love for the most part is elusive and regularly disappoints.

I thought, in bed, of a holiday I had taken with Leo to the Algarve. He played golf all day, every day, and got drunk every night and I got prickly heat from the relentless Mediterranean sun. It was not, by almost any standard, a successful or romantic holiday. I hope Grace has a better time in Paris than I had in Portugal.

Tuesday 22nd January

I endured the flower shop and Mrs. Pratt all morning. She and Jim had been away to Bournemouth with the Caravan

Club for the weekend. They had had, it seems, a wonderful party on Saturday night with everyone getting very drunk. She insinuated that the goings on after that would make my hair stand on end. She laughed so loud and long at the thought of it all I thought she might have temporarily taken leave of her senses.

During my supper I thought about Peter Mallet. What had I to go on? He was an English Language teacher of 39 (?) lately returned from the Far East and living in the periphery of Nottingham, and he wrote with a biro. I felt now, knowing a little about him, that expectations of a soul-meeting, or even physical desire, were minimal. I have found since re-singled not to expect anything from anyone. From this premise when something good happens it is a bonus not an inevitability. Obviously it diminishes or excludes the pleasure of anticipation but that is, I feel, preferable to the constant disappointments that people inflict upon each other.

I had another try with Proust tonight. I feel now, halfway through volume one, a certain empathy with him, but even so, for me, he is a trifle verbose.

At 3.12 a.m. the cat from next door gave a loud and horrifying yell, the sound of which awoke me. I expect it was being raped. I couldn't tell from the noise it made whether it was enjoying the experience or finding it an abomination. I fell asleep with the thought that, universally, whether sex is good or bad seems to be a matter of personal inclination.

Wednesday 23rd January

    I awoke with a headache, the result I suppose of too much reading without the now requisite reading glasses. Two aspirins didn't help and Mrs. Pratt, ever garrulous, infuriated me. She had received in this morning's post, she said, a picnic table from a mail order catalogue. Last night, placed in front of the television to accommodate her supper tray, it had caved-in-the-middle and broken its legs. It was, she said, the fault of the government. I couldn't follow her reasoning for this assumption, and didn't even try. I, myself, thought it was the fault of Mrs. Pratt's greediness. If she had had less food on the tray no doubt its legs would still be standing in their proper place. However, as all employees know, should they wish to keep their employment, silence is best preserved whatever the provocation.

    I met Liz briefly for a sandwich in Marks and Spencer. "Gus," she said, "has got a job on a milk round in North Wellchester. He has done very well so far although he only started on Monday." Gus Ely is not noted for his reliability and endurance where jobs are concerned. In actual fact, two weeks in succession is the longest stint I can remember him ever completing. I expect his pink pony tail would disqualify him from the more conservative openings in Wellchester.

    Rodney at breakfast yesterday, she said, had announced that aggressive feminist women should be shot and that everyone "possible" knew that a woman's place was in the home. Liz, reading the Woman's Page of the Guardian at that particular moment, apparently made no answer. I expect

Rodney, smarting from my remarks, was more likely to be referring to me as an aggressive woman than to Liz, but I kept my peace. "Good luck tonight," she said as we parted. "Remember people who have been out East for any length of time often behave in singularly un-British ways when they come home. This is just a little warning; be on your guard." Did she think Peter Mallet was going to throw me to the ground and rape me in Bar of the Crown Hotel, as Arabs in Girls' Own stories are the Lounge supposed to do? Liz's whole approach to life is one of suspicion, and most of her information is inaccurate. God knows where she gets it from - the Woman's Page in the Guardian newspaper. It is possible that perhaps working in a library subject one to unbalancing stress, although Philip Larkin seems to have kept his sanity tolerably well.

    I met Peter Mallet at the Crown Hotel. He was very small, brown and balding, and if he was 39 I am not yet 30, although I have heard it said that years spent under an Eastern sky age you. In actual fact although looks are not, for me, of any real consequence, conversation, conversely, is. Peter Mallet is a very BORING man. Probably, in truth, the most boring man I've ever had to spend an evening with. He even managed to make the Bedouins sound dull and he had never heard of Suffi poetry or philosophy. I was right about the English Language. He taught fundamental English grammar to Sheiks' spoilt children. With this knowledge, they will I assume on reaching maturity, be able to telephone Harrods from Saudi Arabia to order black silk sheets, or French truffles. Or even perhaps command English women to be sent over, since it is said that Harrods can supply anything whatsoever that a customer desires.

Personally, I think Harrods is quite unspeakable. I told Peter Mallet that my headache had returned and at 10 o'clock sharp I was home.

In bed I spoke to JC. If, I said, we were to be a good working partnership then His intervention in who I met along the very short road to eternity would have to be better organized. I could not, I stressed, waste any more precious time with dull blockheads such as Peter Mallet. Peter Mallet, for his part, obviously thought that I, too, was very boring. What a truly terrible woman, he was probably thinking, driving his Ford Popular back to Nottingham.

Thursday 24th January

Father Murphy called just after I came back from work. There was to be an evening lecture at Blackfriars next Monday evening, he said, on "The Enlightenment" with special emphasis on mid-18th-century Sceptics. The lecturer was to be a Roman Catholic priest, one Father O'Brien. "I expect his knowledge of the Enlightenment is tip-top," I said, "but what, I wonder, is he enlightened about in 1985? What does he think about birth control or abortion, or at least has he an open mind about modern issues? Have you, indeed, Father Murphy?" "Look Missus," said Father Murphy, " can I count on you to come or not? The tickets are £1.20 each, and the proceeds go to the Catholic Missions Overseas." To get him gone I said I would attend the lecture and bought a ticket. I wonder whether he has investments in the Catholic Missions Overseas. He certainly should for the amount of work he does on their behalf. In actual fact I think he pockets some of the money he collects and spends it in the lounge bar at the Wellchester Arms, a place he is fond of visiting, whenever possible.

I have lost 3 lbs. since Saturday but I think it's due to the fact that I've got toothache, which makes eating something of a difficulty. I shall have to visit the dentist. I know from previous experience, captive in the chair, mouth stuck open with revolting pieces of dry cotton wool and metal instruments of torture wound round my teeth, he will tell me of Father's problems with his dentures. And there will be absolutely nothing I can do to stop the flow. Would false teeth be a solution to constant anxiety about dental visits, I wonder?

Diana Cassington-Mackenzie rang to say she was coming to Wellchester next Tuesday. She said in a bossy tone that she was going to visit me for an early supper and then drive to her London flat. She is, no doubt, in need of an audience for her skiing stories and I know that the "audience role" is a part in which I am expert and thus continually asked to play. For supper I said I would cook haddock.

Friday 25th January

I dreamt last night that Leo was having an affair with Mrs. Pratt. I saw them together in the lounge bar of the Crown Hotel. Mrs. Pratt, apparently drinking gin and lemon, was wearing an off-shoulder black satin dress with a large red rose in her hair. She did, of course, look absurd. Leo, I recall, always looked a trifle absurd, and in my dream he hadn't changed. I awoke thankfully to find that I was alone in 11 Maplewood Road. God knows, I thought on the way to work, single life may not be all that we wish for, but for my part, I would choose it every time rather than remain in an intolerable marriage.

I fetched my glasses from John Cassels. Yes I can see better with them, the small print is no longer a blur, but at what sacrifice? Is it only me that resents this particular aspect of the ageing process so very much? If your face is no longer your fortune, as it were, what does it matter whether glasses are an essential or not? I shall have to ask J.C. for guidance on this matter, as it seems to me that I am reacting in a way that is even incomprehensible to me. Perhaps I remember a saying learnt at school those many years ago about "men never making passes at girls who wore glasses." I do remember that well known joke in films where a bespectacled woman of apparently no beauty whatsoever, suddenly has her glasses snatched off by the HERO and hey presto she does, in truth, look like Marilyn Monroe. But since I don't look like Marilyn Monroe or any such a one, with or without spectacles, it doesn't seem personally relevant. My unhappiness about it all must be out of proportion to the actual changes and effects it will have on my life and I am eager for understanding counsel from the Senior Partner. But I suppose since He died at 33 he didn't need reading glasses Himself and, as He could spot his disciples at great distances, I expect He wasn't short-sighted either. Anyway vanity for Him was not, I assume, a problem.

Saturday 26th January

For the sum of £4 I hired a table at a car boot sale in Cuckbury Village Hall. Recycling jumble is, it seems, quite a profitable way of making a few pounds and, since the bills for heating and electricity arrived this week and I have few funds to pay them I decided to join the hopeful ranks of jumble sellers. Amongst other things, I sold three velvet pinafore dresses. The woman who bought them thought they would be suitable to wear in her teashop and confided that she knew she looked young for her 49 years and these dresses would extend (?) the myth. I agreed she looked young for her years - after all she was buying the dresses for £7 each. I felt curiously sad about parting with them as they had been made for me in affluent married days when occasions to wear them had been numerous. I had worn them to parties when Leo's publishing friends had occasion to celebrate best-selling novels. To end their days in a teashop seemed incongruous somehow, as though I had betrayed them. But I came home triumphant. I had made £37, and acquired a blue corduroy waistcoat I swopped for a black jersey with a rival stall holder.

I rang Blueberry Rise and matron said father had developed digestive troubles. However she said his teeth were apparently settling in and knowing father as I do he will certainly need something new to complain about. His digestive tract has always been a source of interest to him.

Although I dislike the television in principle, I watched a recommended film called "East out of Egypt" by way of entertainment after supper. The local paper's T.V. critic, one

Dennis Coles, had obviously enjoyed it otherwise he wouldn't have suggested to his readers that we spend two and a half hours on a Saturday evening watching it. But why he did so is beyond me. Arabs and Indians and Dervishes too I daresay rushed about in dark alleys while officious British army officers shouted orders. As far as I could tell these orders were never carried out, possibly because this army didn't appear to have any MEN in it, and , as we know, it is never the generals who perform the bloody and dangerous deeds in war - they just give the orders and pour themselves another whisky. However idealists strive for equality, I suspect in the order of things that, inevitably, the powerful will always command the powerless and be obeyed. I believe it's called jungle law.

Sunday 27th January

I decided to abstain from the Cathedral's cold portals today and listened to the morning service in bed. It came from a Methodist church in Wales and was full of gloom. All threats of fire and brimstone. No wonder the populace, who in the late 20th-century can choose to go or not to go to church, chose the latter. They prefer no doubt to stay in bed and listen to the sounds of the sixties, or radio 1 or even Letter from America. Or perhaps they make love as an alternative to a spiritual uplift.

Anyway whatever it is they do does not include hurrying to a morning service. I drove to the canal in the afternoon and stood on a bridge watching the barges go by. They are now almost universally brightly painted, and it is difficult to believe that they once carried coal along the waterways. Walking down the towpath I reflected on my single life. I concluded that despite the lack of money, the lack of sleep, and the loss of identity which seems to be part of the lifestyle I had opted for, being captain of my ship instead of 3rd mate was a definite improvement and that the distressing and almost impossible choice I had made was the right one.

Monday 28th January

Today there was a bus strike. I had to walk to work and was late arriving in consequence. Mrs. Pratt was displeased and sharply told me to wash the floors and clean the outside dustbins. She is frequently sharp on Monday mornings, nursing, I suspect, large hangovers. She had purchased over the weekend a truly horrible plastic tree which she hoped to resell at, she said, a considerable profit. For my part it seemed inconceivable that anyone would buy this embodiment of bad taste, but I know my aestheticism is hardly universal and perhaps someone will see it, want it and buy it. Who knows?

Tom rang to say he would be coming to stay on Friday 8th, and would not bring Cathy as she had revision to do. Cathy is, I assume, his new girlfriend. I feel a great relief that he is coming on his own since I see him so little and long to hear his news without any distractions. Leo and Grace will be in Paris in early February, a time of year not known for its good weather - rain, snow, fog and suchlike normally abound, I'm told. Like me perhaps, Grace dislikes the heat and chose Paris in February as a certainty for avoiding heat rash.

Matron at Blueberry Rise said father had been making trouble with Mr. Fently the occupant of the adjacent bed. Father accused Mr. Fently of using his Old Spice After Shave. Since he could smell it on him, he positively knew this to be so. Mr. Fently denied the charge and said father was a lying old bully and he wanted to know nothing of him. Mr. Fently has justly summoned Father up, and I sympathize with him entirely. I remembered in bed that I had forgotten to attend the lecture at Blackfriars on The Enlightenment. Father M. will no doubt call with remonstrations.

Tuesday 29th January

Mrs. Pratt had a cold this morning which precluded much conversation and I found myself, not in the Christian spirit, wishing this condition was a permanent one. She did manage to mention, however, that Prince Edward was going the way of Prince Andrew "if I followed her meaning." Loose women, discos, and general bawdiness was his lifestyle and "where would it all lead to," she croaked. "God knows," I answered, "but I have heard that Prince Edward is homosexual." In actual fact I had heard no such thing. No doubt prince Edward behaves in a similar way to any other young man of 27 who is rich and spoilt or even, indeed, who is not.

    Diana Cassington-Mackenzie came to supper. She was overflowing with gossip - it seeped out of her like a burst water main. Apparently Leo, a friend of Henry Cassington-Mackenzie's, and Grace had dined with them in London last week. Grace, Diana said, was in her late 30s, pretty and petulant. Diana thought Leo might have made a rash decision in his new alignment "although," she added, "one has to remember, Victoria, that Grace is very well endowed, which is a high spade card." Diana frequently makes bridge allusions, most of which I don't understand, but I understood that one. She saved the most exciting news until after the haddock when she said, in some agitation, that in Davos she had met a married man skiing without his wife, who didn't care for the sport. They had danced together in a night spot and frisson had been experienced by both parties it seems. On his return to London, he is going to telephone her. The anticipation of this call gives Diana something to look forward to, but for my part, knowing the realities of life better than Diana, I do not expect him to even remember her name let alone her telephone number. If this man does not contact her, I might drop hints about Rodney Ely.

    I enjoyed the haddock but I don't think Diana did. It reminded her of school, she said.

Wednesday 30th January

This morning I had a bill from the Gas Board for £272.32p. I felt completely sick and drank a drop of whisky. I keep a bottle, as a final resort, to drink on those nights when sleep eludes me completely until dawn and I wake exhausted. How had this ghastly sum accumulated, I asked myself? The gas was installed when I bought the house in November and I remember the plumber explaining the thermostat system. But, not wishing to appear stupid when he explained its workings which I simply did not understand, I said nothing. And now, I found examining the dials, I had run the heating all night in addition to the four hours it was set to work during the day. God, I am such an idiot - how could I be so stupid? "Listen, JC," I said in floods of tears, "You are supposed to look after me, aren't you? So where were You when I should have been wise and was, instead, foolish?" Something will have been learnt I suppose but it is difficult to see, today, what exactly.

I have £400 savings in the Building Society out of which I will take the money owed and settle the account. The week's course I planned to attend in July on Russian Writers in the 19th century is no longer a possibility. Could the lesson, I wonder, be to acknowledge one's weaknesses and not pretend to understand that which one does not?

Thursday 31st January

    Liz and I had lunch at the new Art Centre which has been fashioned out of the old Methodist Church in Lower Pitmarsh. Liz, for a bit of an adventure she said, tried a vegetarian salad consisting of bean sprouts, rice, red kidney beans, dates and nuts. She felt, she said, a little risqué trying something other than a piece of celery quiche. Another adventure she had tried was with her hair, which looked very odd. She had, at her weekly appointment in Debenhams Hair and Beauty Salon, had it coloured with a dark red henna dye. The assistant was obviously not in possession of the expertise needed for this operation since Liz's hair was now mottled, hennaed only in patches. When asked my opinion of it I said it looked very nice because, I tell my conscience - although it certainly did not - telling her the truth would have been inappropriate and unkind.
    Gus, apparently, had found a 5a.m. start for the milk round too much to endure and had, therefore, discontinued his employment on Saturday last. Liz despaired of him and hoped that he wouldn't impregnate Linda (his girlfriend who worked part-time in the Regal Cinema's bar), now that his afternoons were free again. Liz declared that for Gus, sex in the afternoon was optimum and as, she added, at 19 potency sex is at its height, she could foresee trouble. I must say I agree with Gus, sex in the afternoon is most convivial, but, since Liz I felt knew nothing of this pleasure I brought the discussion to a close, and asked after her mother, a safer subject.

I made a delicious supper for myself. Pork chops baked in cider with apple sauce followed by Greek yoghurt and treacle. As I ate it I listened to the Archers and after a few missed weeks I recalled my horror of Peggy Archer. Was there ever such a woman for being truly and consistently irritating beyond what is legitimate? Even Leo's mother, who was quite insufferable, seemed almost possible in comparison. If I was Pat, Peggy's daughter-in-law, I would have bound and gagged her years ago and thrown her body into one of Eddy Grundy's swamps. Forgive me J.C. for this singular lack of tolerance, but some things are for us all, beyond endurance.

Friday 1st February

Mrs. Pratt's granddaughter, Karen, has been taken to hospital in Derby with suspected appendicitis. Mrs. Pratt is therefore going up to stay with her daughter, to comfort and assist her. Could I look after the shop by myself on Monday and possibly Tuesday if she hadn't returned, she asked me. Of course I could, I said, but I would shut the shop at four o'clock after the late deliveries had arrived.

I bought on the way home at Stocks Garden Centre in Blue Street a recommended substance to, it stated, deter cats from using my garden as a public lavatory. Somehow the garden in 11 Maplewood Road has great attraction for all the cats in West Wellchester. It must, of course, be a comfort to the owners of these cats to know that they are not destroying plants in their own gardens or defecating in their treasured lavender bushes. However, they are in mine and I feel an anger hitherto unknown and alien to me against these animals. Perhaps my reaction is out of proportion to the crime, but every plant in my garden was lovingly planted and in addition, paid for by hard work, and many are now torn, broken and do, in fact, smell strongly of cat shit. Is this right, I ask myself? To find the answer should I apply John Stuart Mill's utilitarian principle of happiness - the greatest good for the greatest number? On this premise if there are a) more cat owners than otherwise should they be allowed to let their pets roam at will and b) (nothing to do with J.S. Mill) who am I to complain as a minority vote?

    I dreamt that Mr. Patel from No 13 shot six cats with an automatic rifle when they plagued him. In this one particular instance, I think the reality of this vision is an improvement on the fantasy.

Saturday 2nd February

    I saw Rodney Ely in Smiths buying a copy of the Playboy magazine. He is, I suppose, going through the male menopause. He wishes, no doubt, that the magic of youth would return to him, and wonders where the fire and passion of his loins has gone, and whether that remembered exquisite pleasure is now extinct. He probably knows within himself that making do with Liz once a week or less is now his only portion. Did men, I wonder, in the Augustan Age or in the Renaissance or in Victoria's reign have the same problem? I have no evidence of it in perused history books, if it was so. I shall say nothing to Liz about this sighting although I remember her jokingly saying only two weeks ago that it was lucky for Rodney that Gus's pornographic magazines had not been found under their marital bed. It is strange how near the truth often is, yet of it we are totally unaware.

It was very cold this afternoon and I lit the fire and, sitting by it, abandoning Proust temporarily, I read Jane Austen. Sense and Sensibility was my choice and once again I was astonished at her correct perception of human nature, with all its follies exposed.

Sunday 3rd February

The heating in the Cathedral was only partially working today and, although still cold, it was some improvement on none at all when it is impossible to concentrate, pray, or even think without a struggle. When it is not on at all survival takes all one's energy and application. The Bishop of Grimsby had come to preach and his text was from Revelation, Chapter 1, the bit about the Alpha and the Omega. The Bishop was a dull and ponderous man, lacking inspiration I felt, as my thoughts wandered. The beginning and the end is understandable but the vexing part is the bit in the middle. That is more difficult. The ten commandments are excellent pointers as far as They go, but what is the right or moral argument for or against say abortion, or euthanasia or who should do the washing-up when both partners work? The answers to these questions are not immediately apparent to me, and I am sure that I am not alone in my doubts. The Church's ministers appear to be divided on these matters and if they, divinely guided I hope and presume, cannot make united decisions, how on earth are we lesser mortals supposed to conduct ourselves as God would wish us to?

I spoke to Rodney on the way out who said he was in complete agreement with the Bishop about modern day morality, or the lack of it. Yes, I thought, I bet you are, especially after perusing the Playboy magazine yesterday afternoon when, no doubt, you had told Liz you were in need of fresh air and a walk by the canal. It is not original, I know, to find that nothing is what it seems and nobody is exactly what they appear to be. But it is, nevertheless, a fact.

Monday 4th February

Today was unique. Being responsible for the shop gave me a sense of authority beyond that of a mere employee. Mrs. Pratt telephoned to say she would stay in Derby until Wednesday. For my part I would be thankful if she stayed there all the week; even the plants and flowers seem brighter in her absence.

At noon a tall, well-favoured man came into the shop. He wished to purchase flowers to take to his parents who were staying at The Crown Hotel on a visit to England from Tuscany where, apparently, they now lived. At lunch he was to meet them for the first time in four years. His obvious nervousness at this prospect made him more talkative, I suspect, than he would have been otherwise. With my help, he chose dark red chrysanthemums and two bunches of white narcissi, early blooms from the Isles of Scilly. I mentioned my love of daffodils and their recrudescent messages of spring, at which sentiment he stated that he, himself, hated them. "I teach English," he said, "and every year try to rearrange the curriculum so that Wordsworth's daffodils are not included in the set reading. But somehow I never quite manage it, and I'm afraid my heart does NOT with pleasure fill thinking of the daffodil." I smiled and wished him well with his parents, and thanking me for my help he hurried away to The Crown. Alone and busy, not only my hands but my thoughts were fully occupied until four o'clock and closing time.

9.45. Why can't I stop thinking about that man I ask myself? What was it about him: the John Lennon glasses, the corduroy shirt, the quiet slightly teasing voice or what? Or was it because he was an English teacher, an occupation which women suppose, rightly or wrongly, requires more sensitivity than the average British male possesses. Someone with whom, even if Wordsworth was not a favourite, one could discuss Mrs. Gaskell or Jane Austen perhaps? Or was it simply that I felt attracted to him physically? I do not know, and time, I hope, will tell. I ate a revolting Health Food Crunchy Bar and fell asleep still wondering.

Tuesday 5th February

An order came through for a wedding bouquet which I managed to assemble and dispatch. But the bow to be tied in a yellow ribbon was quite beyond my artistic ability and its drooping appearance somewhat spoiled the total effect. The shop itself became a sanctuary today. The flowers, and the silence, were perfect background for my thoughts, which were filled with The Man Who Bought the Chrysanthemums yesterday.

Father Murphy was lurking outside No 11 Maplewood Road when I got home. I invited him in to tea, which he accepted with alacrity. "Where were you last night, Missus?" he said. "A seat was reserved for you in Row G at Blackfriars, which you did not occupy. I am most disappointed in you. This lack of reliability is just another facet of female aggression that I suggest seethes within you." Briefly we discussed my short-comings until he was reminded of a matter more compelling. It appears that a monk he knew who lived in a monastery outside Gloucester had, after succumbing to sexual temptation with a female member of the kitchen staff, taken his own life, by suffocation. "For myself," said Father Murphy, "I think this a bit extreme. It is generally known," he said, "that contemporary women throw themselves at, and upon, any man they can find. I think it is astonishing," he continued, "that many more men are not seduced by these libertines." "It is possible that this information is generally known, Father Murphy," said I, "However I know of no such women, nor do I believe they exist." Father Murphy left, wishing, no doubt, that he could meet a woman of libertine pretensions in the lounge bar at the Wellchester Arms, his next likely destination.

The Man Who Bought the Chrysanthemums still dominated my thoughts. "JC" I said, "could you see your way to arrange another meeting with this man for me? If you do so I promise I will visit Father over the weekend. And, by the way, this is a bargain not a blackmail."

Wednesday 6th February

Mrs. Pratt, back from Derby, was garrulous beyond what I thought possible, even for her. In fact, she talked, only pausing to take breath, from 9 o'clock until 1 o'clock. I listened only to the general drift which seemed to be that Karen, having had her appendix out on Monday, was now better and returning home tomorrow. Mr. and Mrs. Pratt proposed travelling back to Derby at the weekend. This piece of information took approximately three and a half hours to divulge. Men, I know, are fond of discourse (their own) and frequently dominate conversations in mixed company with dull revelations of their various successes, themselves, or anything else that interest them, regardless of an unenthusiastic audience. However, nothing, I think, can beat the female equivalent of these men. Words tumble from her lips as the rats tumbled after the Pied Piper, in mindless flight. It is no wonder most men wedded to this particular type of woman fall silent early in the partnership and eventually give up altogether. The uncomprehending and insensitive wife then complains that her husband never speaks, and disharmony prevails indefinitely.

Guy Bell telephoned and asked me to have dinner with him on Wednesday February 20th, after a meeting he has to attend in Wellchester. As The Man Who Bought the Chrysanthemums is, after all, insubstantial, I agreed to do so with a modicum of anticipatory pleasure. I shall have to experiment with hair dye preparations to cover the now noticeable grey hairs appearing at my temples. Ageing gracefully does not include, in my opinion, "going grey."

Thursday 7th February

For lunch I has asked Liz to meet me in the lounge bar of the Crown Hotel. She, however, said she did not approve of bars or public houses and incidentally Rodney would not like her to frequent them either. "I will meet you in Poppy's Tea Room," she said, "at one o'clock sharp." Every time Liz tells me what Rodney approves of or does not approve of, I feel uncomfortable, knowing I suppose something of his private inclinations, which are the antithesis of his public image. Is hypocrisy an absolute necessity for civilized life, as it is understood, to progress smoothly, I wonder? Sadly the answer seems to be in the affirmative, and, like others guilty of it, I, myself, am no less so. Liz said Gus was bored with England, and Wellchester in particular, and was going to hitch round India in the summer. Once there he was going to busk if jobless, and had expressed some ambition to teach villagers the English language. I must confess that the idea of Gus teaching anyone the English Language is quite astonishing since, for my part, I have only ever heard him grunt or swear. Neither of these skills would be useful, I think, to rural Hindus or Sikhs. However, I know nothing of India or Indians and am, therefore, no judge of their needs.

    I told Liz about The Man Who Bought the Chrysanthemums. She was not much impressed and said looks were unreliable pointers to character, and that I had simply taken to him with the idea of English Literature, and poetry in particular, equalling a romantic inclination. She said, with her extensive knowledge of teachers (she knows two), that they were often disagreeable, and prone to displays of bad temper and extreme selfishness. I mildly said that perhaps this was a somewhat large generalization and, anyway, it was not important since I wasn't expecting to see him again. Only hoping.

    Matron telephoned from Blueberry Rise. Father had been moved into a single room since nobody in the home wished to share with him, or he with them. Mr. Fently had written to the Board of Governors requesting his removal altogether. On Saturday if Tom and I visit I will take Mr. Fently a small bottle of Johnny Walker whisky, as a bribe to forgive Father. What would I do with father, dear Lord, if he became Old Homeless?

Friday 8th February

In the Arts Centre this afternoon I saw The Man Who Bought the Chrysanthemums. He was viewing paintings - as was I - produced yearly by local artists to raise money for the Cathedral. He, recognizing me, introduced his parents, who were with him. We walked round the exhibition together and he then suggested afternoon tea. In the restaurant, for the sum of £2.50, a special tea was available with scones, strawberry jam and Devonshire clotted cream. This we all chose. (Strangely my diet had gone out of my head.) Colonel Trevelyan, his father, was a smaller version of the son with an engaging smile and friendly, kind eyes. His mother was peaceful and faraway, gathering material, no doubt, in her mind for her next novel. Apparently she wrote many novels none of which were published, but this adversity did not deter her in the least. She wrote simply, she said, because she liked writing. Mark Trevelyan was the son's name. He asked me my name. "It is Victoria Scott," I said, and saw from my watch face that it was exactly 4.17. Mother, before she died, disclosed my time of birth as 4.17 on a Friday afternoon in 1942. I do believe in pre-determination, and think and hope meeting Mark is part of God's larger plan. The Plan of which we have no knowledge and require Faith to believe in, or, at least, to believe that it is a Good Plan even if it does not have the appearance of being so.

Mark was to drive his parents back to The Crown Hotel as they were leaving on the morrow for Italy. As we said goodbye Mark said since real spring daffodils would soon be on sale in the shop he would come in and buy me a bunch. Will he really do so, I wonder.

I played a Nana Mouskouri tape during supper, staring into space. It was eight o'clock before I remembered that I had not tuned into the Archer dynasty. "JC." I said, "It must be something serious for me to forget Ambridge. God knows - well You know anyway - how I hate to miss the daily happenings."

Tom came home, late of course, with all his washing and some of Cathy's, unless he has become a transvestite.

Saturday 9th February

At 12.30 Tom and I had brunch. Toast, marmalade, kippers, fresh coffee, orange juice and cereals. It was delicious, a vast improvement on the healthy yoghurt and prunes I sometimes consume. He was enjoying his first year at Sussex University, he said. The P.P.E. course was not too exacting and gave him time to play rugger, a game at which he excelled. His girlfriend Cathy was studying classics, but apart from this practical information, I learnt nothing about her of an intimate nature. Perhaps he will disclose more tomorrow.

But I do now know more of Grace. She is a more suitable partner for Leo than I was apparently, since she does in fact LIKE parties, and noise, and public school prats and fast cars and money. I agreed that if this were so then she would be the very partner Leo craved, and had found wanting in myself. She is not, it seems domesticated, cooking being the least of her inclinations, and therefore they dine out more than they dine in. Not a question, then, of plus ça change. How much easier, I reflected, it seems for a re-singled man to find a suitable mate than it does for a re-singled woman. Perhaps men's list of priorities is very different from women's, their list of essential qualities less demanding. Do they think when realigning themselves: if she is presentable, willing in bed and can cook, what more do I need? Tom says Grace calls Leo Leokins which he professes to like. "It all sounds very satisfactory," I said, "I am glad to hear that they are happy." But, curiously, that sentiment was not exactly the truth.

 We decided to visit father tomorrow, and went this afternoon to a film of Tom's choice, something about Vietnam. I, myself, hate films about war. I went to sleep and awoke at its end to see a battlefield full of dead soldiers. Tom, as we left, said he thought it an excellent film, abounding in action and excitement. Obviously I couldn't agree since action and excitement are two things I, myself, never seek.

 This evening Tom spent twenty-five minutes on the telephone to Cathy. I do believe most children think telephone calls are free, and that they themselves are in no way responsible for the large account their parents have to pay at the end of the quarter. Why am I so reluctant to point out this fundamental error to my children? Because, I suspect, it would sound parsimonious.

Sunday 10th February

This morning, in return for doing his washing and ironing, Tom came to the Cathedral with me. Tom thinks God is a consolation to the middle-aged, and a necessity for those getting nearer their time to meet Him. But for himself, since he imagines he has many years in credit, he frankly admits to disbelief and indifference. Anyway, he came. I saw Rodney and Liz (no Gus) three seats in front of us. Looking at them objectively they appeared to be the perfect, respectable married couple. Who would know, I thought, of Rodney's secret aspirations, or his desires for a renaissance of sorts. It is thought by the uninitiated that church goers are removed from the temptation of their peers. A thought which is, of course, absurd, since their flesh is, in truth, just as weak as the next man's, or weaker if the Sunday tabloids are to be believed. The sermon was unmemorable and anyway I worried throughout as I could not remember shutting the front door. I am always worrying about shutting the front door, which is strange since I have never yet left it open, and cannot imagine doing so.

We went to visit father. He was not particularly pleased to see us. He did not like being in a room on his own, he said it gave rise to talk when he was alone with the nurse, one Mrs. Hill, who gave him his bed baths. Tom, who had seen Mrs. Hill, said he thought it most unlikely that anyone could get sexually aroused by her, to which Father said Tom was vulgar beyond everything. "And anyway," he said petulantly, "we are supposed to be talking about me." Most people, it is certain, prefer talking themselves than listening to others doing so. So much talking takes place, I thought, so many words and so few of them worth listening to. After tea we went home. The visit, I concluded, had not been a success.

At 7.05 Tom took the coach back to Brighton and I cleaned the bath. JC, I prayed, while doing so, "will you arrange for Mark Trevelyan to keep his word to come to the shop and buy me daffodils? Soon."

Monday 11th February

I made an appointment at 3.30 on Friday afternoon, to see Dr Miles. The recurring pains in my hands and behind my eyes are still a worry. Being my own physician is losing its appeal since the many diverse medications I buy have, it seems, no success whatsoever.

On Saturday night Mrs. Pratt had been to a dinner-dance in Marlborough organized by the Caravan Touring Club. The evening had been a great success, she said. A local cabaret singer with something of Des O'Connor's appeal had been hired to entertain, which he did admirably, obliging with all the old favourite songs. For herself, Mrs. Pratt said, her favourite song was "Danny Boy," a song which I recall John F. Kennedy enjoyed. Predictably at this point in Mrs. Pratt's Saturday night stories, the Caravan Club members all got a trifle drunk, and she hinted at a certain amount of excitement dancing close with an old admirer of hers, one Terry McGough. Terry McGough was, she explained, a telephone engineer. She has booked herself an appointment at Clare's Salon for a perm and I wonder whether she is experiencing the same desire for lost youth as Rodney Ely. Indeed, am I experiencing it myself? Certainly my own behaviour of late has been quite singular for a sensible middle-aged lady.

I bought two plants home from the shop. Both of the green leaf variety, which even I will find it hard to kill, immediately anyway.

Tuesday 12th February

At 8 a.m. Diana telephoned. Henry was being more dull and difficult than usual (is that possible?) and the man from Davos, on whom she had pinned her hopes, had not telephoned. Why had he not, she asked, and did I think he would eventually, or should she give up hope, and many similar questions poured forth. "No," I said, "I do not think he will. Holiday romances are not known for their reliability or endurance after the reality of life returns, once home. But when you next come to Wellchester I know a man who might just suit you. He has a dull marriage in which he naturally wishes to remain, but nevertheless would like a little excitement injected into his day. And as I think your requirements are much the same, suitable arrangements could perhaps be made." I told her Rodney wasn't top drawer material but pointed out that Diana was not in a position to make choices. She agreed she was not and I promised to approach Rodney about a meeting.

I felt uneasy when I replaced the receiver. How, I asked myself, if Liz is supposed to be a true friend of mind could I possibly think of Diana and Rodney, her husband, enjoying an extramarital affair? It was a thoughtless and stupid idea of mine and in addition morally unacceptable. I shall have to think of any alternative. Perhaps Diana would like Guy Bell? At least they would have the love of wind-surfing in common, and his dog. Diana likes dogs.

Wednesday 13th February

The forecast snow fell in the night and it was bitterly cold today. The bus to work was full of people looking miserable - even the bus chatterers were silent. How I wish I dared tell them about starting the day with hot porridge. I am sure with a hot-porridge-start their lives would be less intolerable. But my courage failed me and I left the bus silently. On reflection, I am glad I wasn't born a man and expected to serve my country. I know, although it has never been put to the test, that I am a coward, and perhaps this is why I admire courage in my fellows above other virtues.

That evening I feel lonely. It was lovely seeing Tom and I realize how much I miss the children. I spoke to Harriet last week. She was working hard and enjoying sharing the Hackney flat with Penny and Charlotte. Musing, I re-read the Renoir postcard I had had from Sarah stating her intention to come here on Saturday afternoon. Memories of my children's childhood filtered through my mind. I thought of how much they had tried my patience, and how often, and yet how much I loved them. With this mournful mood upon me I have just poured myself a large gin and tonic and propose to consume several more before this night ends.

Hello, JC it's me. Please guide me to the front door before I go to bed and see that I lock it.

ST VALENTINE'S DAY
Thursday 14th February

Perhaps I have been unfair about the romantic nature of Englishmen. Today they poured into the shop to purchase bunches of flowers for their wives and single roses for their lovers, mistresses or girlfriends. I was envying the recipients of these posies when Mark came into the shop. Knowing my romantic inclinations, he said, and today being St Valentine's Day, he thought it would be appropriate to come in and buy me a bunch of daffodils. He bought me white narcissi and, as he left, he asked for my telephone number. I wrote it in haste, on the back of a bereavement card, the nearest thing I could find.

As the door closed Mrs. Pratt said that it was not permissible for staff to flirt with customers. It was not businesslike, she said, and moreover people might gain the wrong impression about her shop. "This is not, make no mistake," she said, " a massage parlour." Mrs. Pratt is absurd. When her mind is not full of Royal gossip, it is full of the sexual activities in which she imagines others participate and, of late, in which I think she wishes to participate herself. Her hair is now the colour of vanilla ice cream and I wonder whether Terry McGough will care, or even notice. Perhaps Mrs. Pratt is unaware of the following cliche and should add it to her formidable collection: that you don't have to look at the mantlepiece when you are poking the fire. I might tell her of it.

I thought about Mark and the possibilities thereof all evening and, for no particular reason, I made a chocolate cake. The daffodils he gave me are in a white china jug on my bedside table, and spring, surely, is in the air.

Friday 15th February

My visit to Dr Miles was not a success. I still know nothing particular about my worrying aches and pains. They could be a variety of things apparently, vis: arthritis, the beginning of the menopause, lying in a draft, or even the lack of this or too much of something else. What this was I did not gather and, it seems, the doctor did not know. In short, the doctor has no more idea of the origins of these pains or how long they will continue or when, if ever, they will disappear, than I have. I shall ask Harriet what Mr. Haines gives the animals who visit his surgery with stiff legs and paws. With this information and that which I can collect from reading Medical Health Care books in the library I might chance upon the answers myself. After studying philosophy for a year or two I quite understand that philosophers are allowed to ask questions which do not have answers, or at least no specific answers, and I wonder if doctors' questions run on the same lines. It seems they do.

Matron rang to say Father was on hunger strike and furthermore had locked himself into the only lavatory on the 2nd floor, all the afternoon. His grievance was that he did not wish to occupy a single room. The neglect to himself he said, was horrendous

Saturday 16th February

I worked out a new diet for myself with the help of several books I read on the subject of healthy eating. Incidentally, one of these books suggested that if we did not eat meat, butter, cakes, or chocolates, or drink alcohol (any) or coffee or tea, we would have a long and healthy life. I have no doubt whatsoever that this statement is entirely true but how incredibly boring and dull it sounds. I shall, therefore, take the path of moderation., Sarah arrived before lunch. Liz was here accompanied by Gus who wanted a lift to the Three Elms Public House. Sarah decided that she too would enjoy a drink and they left together, opting to go by bus. Gus, I think, would appeal to Sarah since he is the embodiment of all she holds in high esteem. A punk, a rebel who smokes and drinks too much but is nevertheless clever, and has certain charm. She returned in good humour after five o'clock, and only just managed to catch the 5.30 coach back to Marlborough. She will be back again soon, she said, in fact probably next weekend. Gus then, it appears, pleased her. Did she please him, I wonder, and what of Linda if she did? Not my problem, I decided after some thought.

For the purpose of broadening my mind I discarded Victorian literature this evening and read a book about Hitler and his atrocities. How is it possible for a human being to so behave, I asked myself, completely sickened. "J.C.," I said, "It is very difficult for us to believe in You and Your Total Goodness when you never intervene, even in extreme cases of human folly, when YOU SHOULD."

Sunday 17th February

I slept badly and felt tired this morning. I had dreamt of Leo and Grace dancing together in Sainsbury's. In reality Leo had not been deft on his feet where dancing was concerned and I worried, in the dream, about the consequences of him inadvertently knocking against a full shelf of tinned foods and the whole consignment falling down on top of them.

The first lesson read in the Cathedral today was to do with the Tree of Life (Book of Revelation, Chap. 2), where apparently in Heavenly Jerusalem (our final destination?) there will be no night. This thought for those of us who are not good sleepers and find the night often long and dark, should be a comfort. There will be no more tears or weeping either so for those of us whose hours are sometimes spent thus, Heaven seems a place of promise.

I took Bucket for a walk along the canal or, in truth, he took me. But I had learnt from his disobedience on the previous walk, and, despite his pleading looks, his lead stayed securely attached to his collar. The snow had not completely cleared and it was very cold and very beautiful. The trees and bushes looked like silver cobwebs, and on the canal the small windows in the barges shone with smudgy yellow lights and thick smoke curled out of their chimneys. They appeared snug and inviting. I thought, as I walked, about Mark. My thoughts predictably ran thus: I hope if it is ordained that we are to be partners that in him I can find someone to love in the way that I so wish for and, indeed, in the only way I think of as possible. That is to say with trust and truth.

Monday 18th February

Mrs. Pratt has new fears today. They are about the Queen Mother. In Mrs. Pratt's opinion the Duke of Edinburgh frequently snubs Her Majesty. He turns his back on her at Royal occasions, and when Prince Andrew decides to wed, at his marriage she can visualize the Queen Mother insulted once more. She expanded the theory that since the Duke of Edinburgh was a FOREIGNER, and it is well known that Foreigners are not trustworthy, and mostly dagos to boot. He probably was, in addition, rude and unpleasant to the Queen. Where was he, after all, she wanted to know, the night a man broke into Buckingham Palace? Mrs. Pratt, I gathered, does not like the duke. For her part, she thinks of him as a black sheep and declared that it was well known that through him all the Royal Family's problems descend. She thinks the Queen has much to put up with. I said most families wouldn't mind swopping their life styles for a day or two, with the Royal Family's. I pointed out that the Duke of Edinburgh's behaviour was similar to any other M.C.P. and that the woman of England would recognize him as such and expect the bullying and bad manners. But, I pointed out, at least the Queen doesn't have to iron his shirts, or wash up his breakfast. Presenting this argument, I concluded that the Queen has less to put up with than most people.

    I rushed home hoping Mark would telephone, but he didn't. Liz Ely rang to ask me to meet her for lunch on Thursday. She wanted to discuss something with me, she said, a matter of some importance. Has she found lipstick on Rodney's handkerchief or discovered, when filling his briefcase with lunchtime sandwiches, a copy of Playboy magazine? Or is Gus changing sex, or is she, Liz, after an adventure of her own - something like joining an evening class? Well, whatever it is, excitement abounds and I look forward to revelations on Thursday in the Poppy Tea Room.

Tuesday 19th February

    I have today, I think, invented The Perfect Diet. For the ingredients of this diet I went to Sainsbury's on the bus, and returned laden with vegetables, fruit, prunes, apricots, herbal tea, and sunflower seeds. The kitchen table looked like a health food shop with not a decent chocolate cake or biscuit or jam roll in sight.

    Mark did not telephone this evening and after a somewhat depressing dinner of sardines, raw turnips, carrots and parsnips followed by natural yoghurt I poured myself a large gin and tonic, and took Proust to bed with me.

Wednesday 20th February

Guy Bell took me out to dinner in Marlborough. We went to a small French restaurant. The tables were covered with red and white gingham tablecloths and single carnations stood in glass vases. Candles on saucers were the only lights in the room. A real-life romantic candle-lit dinner, but sadly, with the wrong man. We discussed socialist principles and the Welfare State, two subjects on which I have little real knowledge, and questionable interest. Later we talked of his patients. I asked him what most of them went to see him about. Did they visit him because listening neighbours and friends were a thing of the past, and there was no one else to talk to? Guy implied that my reasoning was not inaccurate and said that if this was indeed so, and it could be, he had no complaints since he himself benefitted. Guy, for me, I thought looking at him while he talked, lacks any kind of magic. Magic that is important to us all, to lighten the greyness of everyday existence, if only for a moment or two. Physically I cannot imagine kissing him, let alone more serious considerations, even after the two drinks which are supposed to release inhibitions.

I offered to pay for my share of the dinner, a gesture which was new to me and rather difficult to voice. I read somewhere that the modern single woman of the 80's is expected to pay her way and if richer than her escort, pay his as well. Guy agreed that my paying half was in order and I gave him exactly £11.27p. A question here surely: having parted with your well-earned money, was the outing worth it? I suspect men of my generation, who always did pay for their companion's dinner or whatever, must have had that thought, frequently. But I suppose, if it was part of a wooing process with total submission in mind, and they ultimately achieved their goal, they might have thought the money well spent. As Mrs. Pratt would say I am sure: "The one who pays the piper calls the tune," a cliche which reveals, as do most cliches, a certain truth.

    I didn't ask Guy in for a drink and got to bed before midnight. Guy, I thought before sleeping, likes playing squash. A man keen on playing squash simply would not do for me at all. I find the thought of squash boring beyond sufferance.

Thursday 21st February

    Liz had a cold and put off our lunch arrangement. We rearranged it for Monday 25th. How will I bear the suspense?

    I bought a box of "Beautiful Black" hair dye from Boots on the way home. The label says it guarantees to make my hair a beautiful colour and, furthermore, condition it and give it a "glossy sheen," all for £2.75p. The woman portrayed in the picture on the box looks witchlike, her hair gypsy black. The colour I suppose mine will turn when the dye is applied.

I do wish Mark would ring me. It is seven days since February 14th and although the daffodils he gave me are now very dead in the china vase beside my bed, I can't throw them away. I left a pleading memo for JC on the kitchen table asking him to quicken events since I find waiting uncertainly very stressful, and as He knows I do not wish or need any more stress in my life. "I have been down that road," as Mrs. Pratt would say, and I, myself, would add that it didn't lead anywhere I wanted to go.

Friday 22nd February

Father Murphy called at four o'clock and I tried him out with the herbal tea. For himself, he said, after tasting the brew, he could well do without herbal tea and asked had I instead a drop of Scotch whisky? He had, that very afternoon, been tempted by flesh in the form of a woman, he said, and was still recovering from the shock. It appears that he has duties at Blackfriars, once a week, which involve serving free teas and coffees to any Pitmarsh resident in need. A certain woman he did not name visited on a regular basis, and constantly engaged him in conversation of a rather racy nature. Not, he told me, in case I had forgotten (how could I?) that because he was a Priest it followed that he didn't know the ways of the world. "I'm up to date with sexual matters, missus," he said "make no mistake."

After a number of free teas and coffees this woman had asked Father Murphy, who had confessed an interest in her stuffed butterfly collection, to visit her. He arrived at the appointed hour for the visit today and she opened the door wearing nothing but a leotard. "My heart raced, missus," he said. "I felt aroused looking at the bare pink flesh of her neck and breasts." Breathless apparently, he excused himself and hurried here. Under these circumstances I poured him a small portion from my bedside whisky bottle. We discussed the undeniable fact that the flesh is indeed weak and I felt closer to Father Murphy than I have ever previously. I hope I comforted him - I certainly tried to do so. I said that the way we are all so astonished when judges, politicians, churchmen, doctors et al are discovered behaving badly in some way (usually sexually) was ridiculous. Temptation is relative, and theirs is no less difficult to resist than anyone else's. The whisky and words calmed Father Murphy and I felt that today we had in some measure, in the soul-saving-stakes, reversed roles.

Saturday 23rd February

Mark telephoned at nine o'clock. I was reading, at the time, a piece concerning badgers from the Countryman's Notes column in the Independent newspaper. It is Wellchester School's half term holiday next week, and we arranged to meet for afternoon tea in the residents' lounge of the Crown Hotel on Wednesday. To the exclusion of everything else I listened to Edith Piaf tapes and the Beatles for the rest of the day, and thought about Mark and felt dizzy.

Sunday 24th February

I awoke at dawn and decided to go to the 8a.m. Holy Communion service. Holy Communion is a very special service for me. I love its purity. and often wish I could take the Bread and Wine in solitude since the unity between myself and Christ, at that moment, seems such an enormous and private emotion. I sometimes wonder whether if I took communion every day my flesh would become more Christlike, nourished by His Body and refreshed by His Blood. And would His Divinity flow through me more with constant attendance at the communion rails, I wonder? It is a thought that interests me, one I think of often.

I listened to an hour of the Archers when I got home. Perhaps Pat Archer should have had that affair she obviously desired with a bearded poly-teacher some years back. She might have sounded less grumpy than she does today if she had something to remember in her life that was more exciting than Tony's organic carrot crop.

Sarah rang. She said she and Gus Ely were meeting in Wellchester next Saturday to join a C.N.D. protest march. She might drop in and she might not. Query: do our children imagine that their parents have no plans of their own, or if they do have plans that they can be dropped, or should be, if they wish to visit home at their convenience, to see us? For my part, my plans for next Saturday have yet to be decided upon, since they rest on hope, not certainty.

Monday 25th February

At lunchtime I met Liz at the Poppy Tea Room. Her news concerned Rodney, and his activities. He had been behaving in an odd way of late, said Liz, taking up jogging every evening, and buying himself articles of clothing not suitable in the least for someone of 46 and a Church Warden. What did I think was going on, she asked. Liz is probably the only woman left in England in 1985 who knows nothing of the male mid-life crisis, and its implications. I told her that Rodney was probably experiencing some of the well-known symptoms and emphasized the need to support him in whatever he did, even if she did think buying jeans and coloured shirts to wear was a trifle absurd at his age. That way, I said, the crisis may never happen and Rodney will settle down again and not re-align himself with a woman half his age, to prove his manhood or whatever it is that needs proving. The thought of Rodney leaving with another upset Liz quite somewhat and she said she would do her best to understand the problem.

I told her I was meeting Mark for tea: how beautiful his voice sounded on the telephone and that, in truth, I had thought of nothing else since Saturday. But she was not very interested. Her memories perhaps of falling in love have blurred into nothingness, and new ones are not wanted, or anticipated by her in the future, and love therefore is not a subject in which she wishes to participate. I shall have to ring Diana. Other people's love affairs, and her own (should she have one) are the food of life to her and a real source of felicity.

Tuesday 26th February

I have lost 2lbs since Saturday. My diet it seems is working but I suspect it is more to do with my state of mind than my will power since I have had, of late, no thoughts whatsoever about fudge, or biscuits or chocolate or condensed milk. In fact I haven't thought about food since Saturday.

What I have selected to wear tomorrow is quite a worry. After much deliberation I have decided upon (from a small selection) the green corduroy skirt, white shirt and green and grey striped jersey, and I have cleaned my black boots and washed a pair of black tights. Are men vain too, I wonder? Do they worry about what they look like, or what they are going to wear on a first date, or both or neither, as much as women or indeed at all? I have not thought about these points before, and have no way of knowing the answer. I knew Thomas Hardy looked sadly into his mirror in his old age and was not pleased with what he saw. He wished to look young again, but that is not quite the same thing. I would guess that vanity is as fairly apportioned to men as it is to women, just less overtly.

Matron rang from Blueberry Rise. Father is on probation in a room with three others. As yet, but he only went there last night, there have been no incidents.

"JC," I said, putting out the light "could you remember to accompany me into the Residents Lounge at the Crown Hotel tomorrow, since the two of us might do better than just me on my own?"

Wednesday 27th February

Today I fell in love taking afternoon tea in the Residents Lounge of the Crown Hotel, Wellchester. No wonder people mistake the way to Paradise since they cannot all know the secret lies in the most direct route into Wellchester High Street, and thence into the Crown Hotel. I want to relive those dizzy moments over tea all my life. Thus I write them down now to remind me lest I, in old age, forget what magic feels like, forget how falling-in-love enhances everything, forget completely how unaware one is of all externals and how totally engrossed one is with the loved one, to the exclusion of all else.

No one else it seemed existed in the tea room. For all I know of it, Mark and I were the only ones there, yet The Crown is popular for tea especially on market day, and I suspect there were others, invisible to myself. Mark had arrived before me. He was in the Residents' Lounge, sitting in a chair by the window; reading a book. He wore brown corduroy trousers, a brown polo neck jersey and an old, old tweed jacket. Quintessentially an Englishman of taste, or at least of my taste.

What did we talk of in the hour that seemed like a minute? It was established, I think, that English literature,

Jane Austen and Thomas Hardy, particular loves of mine, were loves of his too. I am certain he said he had had a wife who left him to "find herself" which she was now doing in Exeter, where she lives with their daughter, Posy. And was it 1983 or 1984 they got divorced? It is difficult to remember exactly what was said as my mind was swirling about at a strange, previously unknown level of consciousness, as if somehow I was removed from myself. Facts were divulged but not sharply taken in; I spoke too, but of what, goodness only knows. Dusk was falling when we stepped into the High Street and Mark touched my cheek briefly with his lips and said, "I will call you soon, Victoria." I know that is exactly what he said as I have repeated it to myself a thousand times since six o'clock and it is now 10.45p.m. and I am tired.

"Thank you for coming with me, JC," I whispered before I turned out the light. "As I predicted, things went well with the two of us there." At 2a.m. - still awake - I remembered that Mark Trevelyan smokes Gauloise cigarettes.

Thursday 28th February

I was hopeless in the shop today. I dropped a china vase with one of Mrs. Pratt's hideous flower arrangements in it, and I added up a woman's bill erroneously forgetting to charge her for two bowls of potted hyacinths. Mrs. Pratt, when she discovered the error, said she would deduct the missing money from my wages. Mrs. Pratt is, I think, a woman of mean temperament.

I bought a book of love poetry from Smiths on my way home. An anthology of poems collected over the centuries, some of which were written by Greek poets before Christ's birth, works of Homer, Virgil and Ovid. The process of love changeth not, then, it seems - it has all been fermenting since the beginning of time; all so old, and yet so new to me. Thoughts elsewhere entirely, I put all my dirty white laundry into the washing machine with a pink T-shirt of Sarah's. Everything now washed is pale pink (candy floss colour) and looks unbearable, and certainly unwearable.

Friday 1st March

This afternoon I applied the "Beautiful Black" hair dye preparation and the result was quite successful. It was much easier than I had anticipated, although unfortunately much of the bathroom carpet, a pale beige, is now also black.

I rang Diana and told her about Mark. She said, a little wistfully I thought, how pleased she was for me, and wished she too was in love. As it was, she said, the man from Davos had not rung and Henry was a shit, which is not a new revelation about her husband. Why are all shits rich, she asked me. The answer was in the question I said and left her to work that out. Diana, I thought, is frivolous and trivial and irritating as only the aristocracy can be, but she is a good friend and I feel great affection for her. As well described in true boarding-school fashion, she is a "good egg"; and infinitely preferable to some of the left-wing feminist women I have met in Wellchester who are, literally, indescribable.

Saturday 2nd March

Sarah arrived as I was eating breakfast wondering how to pay both the electricity and telephone bills this month. If I had to choose between no electricity and no telephone I would settle for candles without hesitation. In my opinion, the telephone is a necessity not a luxury for a person who lives alone. Sarah was meeting Gus at 10.30 outside the Three Elms Public House, the appointed place for the start of the C.N.D. march. Sarah said Gus was "cool," which was more than she could say for the men she met in Marlborough, who were not. Is Linda on the way out and Sarah on the way in I wonder? Query: Should I talk to Sarah about contraception, or does she know more about it than I do? I suspect modern youth knows a number of things about sexual matters that I know nothing of, nor does Father Murphy for that matter, despite his protestations. I think therefore I shall say nothing and hope this is not the coward's way out. IT IS SO DIFFICULT BEING A PARENT.

I took the bus into Wellchester town centre this afternoon and bought myself at Kipper Boutique a full skirt of beige and black wool. It would match my suede jacket and black boots I thought, and dismissed the pricks of conscience about the accumulation of unpaid bills.

Just after five Mark rang me from a call box. Should we go for a walk by the canal tomorrow afternoon, he said. Yes, I said, we should. He is fetching me at 2.30 and my heart is thumping and the hours between now and 2.30 tomorrow seem interminable. How will I get through them? I shall play Beethoven's fifth violin concerto for peace, read Proust to assure myself that love is all consuming, even in middle age, and drink gin because gin silvers the mind (as I once read in a novel) and I love its effect of blurring the edges.

Saturday 3rd March

My attention was not wholly absorbed in the Cathedral today. I have no idea what the sermon was about but I saw Rodney and Liz paying attention so perhaps it was something pertinent to them. People do listen to the sermon throughout (not just the first minute) if it relates to themselves.

Mark fetched me at 2.30, as promised, and we drove down to the canal. It was a lovely fresh early spring day, and everything looked very beautiful, the grass greener, the sky bluer, and even the swans whiter than I had noticed before. We walked down the canal path until there were no more houses or buildings in sight, just stretches of fields and woods. And it seemed once again as if there was nobody else in the world except Mark and me. And on the way back, hours, minutes, days later? he took my hand and we talked of many things, of ourselves, and of love, and why we preferred to shop in Sainsbury's, and why we loved in particular the sound of the westerly winds.

Before I went to bed I wrote these words on the back of an envelope I found in the bedside drawer:

>Today, I, Victoria Scott, have embarked on a New Life. I pray to God that He will endow me with Wisdom and Patience when I encounter the many difficulties that Love must surely bring.

I placed this on the mantlepiece, then made a chocolate drink with full dairy milk, which was, of course, delicious.

Friday 8th March

I told Mrs. Pratt I was in love and it was for this reason, no doubt, that I was being less efficient in my work. Curiously Mrs. Pratt was quite sympathetic when she understood the cause of my inattention. I suspect that inside Mrs. Pratt there lies a romantic heart which would explain her egregious interest in love affairs - particularly the Royal Family's. Most women, I think, are drawn towards tales of love; the mere mention of "Brief Encounter," that universally beloved old romance, brings tears aflowing to the eyes of millions. How is it possible, I wonder, that a film can be so popular without any nude bodies in it, or explicit sex, or indeed any sex? Could it be that romantic heroes are more thrilling than Rambo's? Well, its just a thought ...
Mark and I are going out to dinner tomorrow night, perhaps to the White Hart in Bath. He is to fetch me at 7.15.

Saturday 9th March

    I read a complete Georgette Heyer novel today since I knew I couldn't concentrate on anything more serious. It was as diverting and pleasurable as it had been in my youth. In a complete dither I started to get ready for dinner much too early and wished I was more "laid-back" like my children who, when going out for the evening, don't seem to get ready until two minutes before the appointed time, if then. I bathed and dressed and sprayed myself liberally with expensive scent, a present from Diana, and the clock stood at barely 6.35. In the three quarters of an hour I had to wait I ate a cheese sandwich, played both sides of the Piaff tape, re-applied glossy lipstick, and rang the telephone time machine twice. It was then only 7.05 and I sat in a heap, dizzy, having exhausted all time-filling possibilities until the bell rang. Mark looked very appealing. I like the gold National Health spectacles he wears, the type sported by Ghandi and John Lennon. They are, to me, symbolic, but of what I cannot exactly define. Perhaps it is intellect, and kindness, and a gentle disposition although of course there is no good, or scientific, reason for thinking thus. We did go to the White Hart and sat at a table by a log fire. I felt euphoric, sublime, and what else? Yes, different from anything I had known before and I am 42 years old. I remember thinking, coming back from the Hayes lunch party two months ago, that it was probably impossible to fall in love in middle-age. But here I was middle-aged and in just that state. It is 2a.m. and I am alone writing this in front of dying embers and amongst empty glasses and a full ashtray. I will ask the children if the middle-aged are allowed to adopt student habits if they missed out on this scene the first-time round. Mark, as house-master, has to preside over the boy's breakfast at 7.45, and we are no longer of an age when without sleep, a full working day is possible. He kissed me before he left and I thought (yes I know it is not an original thought) my heart would literally stop beating. God knows (indeed He does) I do not wish for any further maladies, (like a heart attack) and I have therefore sat down here, my head swimming, to think. Age, then, for falling in love is irrelevant it seems. Kissing Mark I felt the same excitement as I did at 15 when I had my first kiss, with my first love. How many in-between years is that? Twenty-eight or nine? And where did they go? The candle's flame has burnt down past the half way mark by middle-age, there are now no years to waste away. Brief candle, indeed. It is 3.17. I shall stagger up to bed. "Thank you JC" I said "for arranging this second chance for me. But I have one worry. I do wish Mark was not agnostic and hope it won't be an issue between us." Bucket barked all night but since I couldn't sleep it didn't matter to me. Although I dare say for those people in the street not smitten by love, Bucket's barking must have been something of a trial.

Sunday 9th March

Miracles really bother me, I reflected, as I sat in the Cathedral this morning. Whenever I hear the lesson from St Matthew C.14 about Christ feeding the multitudes with five loaves and two fishes, the idea seems quite inconceivable. I looked up the word 'miracle' in Cassells Dictionary when I got home and its definition is: "a marvellous event" or "an extraordinary occurrence." In truth feeding five thousand people on what appeared to be just enough supper for four is indeed "an extraordinary occurrence," - in short, a miracle. So how does one accept the "truths" of the Bible when frequently their literal meaning seems so perverse? Mark was on duty all day and in the afternoon I walked by myself along the canal towpath. My being in love, I thought, is a miracle, but a miracle that needs no interpretation. Harriet, Tom and Sarah, if they knew, would think the situation hilarious. Sarah certainly thinks men and women over thirty are geriatrics - wrinkled and pathetic has-beens. On reflection I shall not tell them about Mark until after Easter - or perhaps never. I rang Blueberry Rise. Matron said father was trying to behave in a more convivial manner. I presume from this information that he hasn't bitten the man in the adjacent bed yet. But father's good intentions never last long. He will probably break out next week.

Wednesday 13th March

Mark and I went to the Mallory Music Rooms for a concert. It was Mozart's Piano Concerto in A. We held hands and as I sat still absorbing the music's sweetness, I thought, dear God, can this really be happening to me? Later, at No 11 Mapelewood Road, we ate a cold supper of smoked mackerel, french bread and butter, cheese and fruit.

We drank chilled white wine (not Sancerre). We talked of Hardy's poems and of the grief he felt on the death of his first wife. We discussed how strange it was that during her life he was unfaithful to her, at least in word if not in deed, and was, it seems, totally insensitive to her emotional requirements. Mark said his wife, Anna had been insensitive to his needs, although he did admit that perhaps he, too, had been at fault, unaware of hers. But apparently until the break-up, when she left to "find herself" and her "personal space" (Oh Jane Austen wouldn't you hate these revolting words), nothing was said by either party of their unhappy state. This seems to be a universal malady; non-communication. Certainly on no occasion did Leo and I speak of emotion or, in abstract terms, about anything. Safe subjects were the only ones allowed and possible. Subjects such as love, truth, or happiness were dangerous. Where after all might they lead? To impossible exposure of the self perhaps, and, envisaging this catastrophe, these subjects were forbidden. Mark did not seem too distressed for himself over the divorce but was sad that seeing Posy, his 12-year-old daughter, was difficult. Exeter is a long way from Wellchester and getting there presents problems. Cinderella-like Mark had to be back at school at 11 o'clock, but he is coming to supper here on Saturday night. "And I, Deo Gratis, don't have to appear at breakfast on Sunday morning, this time," he said smiling at me as he left. What does that mean exactly, I wonder? What has he in mind? In truth despite my 42 years I know very little of men's minds. For my part I know when he holds my hand, or touches my lips with his first finger, or when he kisses me, the effect has a devastating impact. Who said something about two drinks and I am anybody's? Totally sober after a cup of mint tea at breakfast I would probably succumb to temptation, with alacrity. I felt like eating a Mars Bar before going to bed but tonight, I found the will power, absent on most occasions, to resist.

Thursday & Friday, 14th & 15th March

My mind and body seem to have disconnected. I do nothing efficiently and everything slowly. Mrs. Pratt says she had an aunt who fell in love in middle age. The aunt, in her state of confusion, fell out of the train in which she was travelling, onto the railway tracks and was killed outright. Taking note, I shall keep away from the railway station in future.

Saturday 16th March

Finally the day came, and went. I decided to cook ox-tail for dinner. Leo had enjoyed the ox-tail I cooked for him over the twenty years we were united in marriage. I had perfected the art of the gravy, he said, an issue of importance in ox-tail stew. I hope Mark liked it as much as Leo did. He said he liked it, but not how much. For the pudding I made apple snow. Apple snow is not, of course, Cordon Bleu, but it is light after richness of the ox-tail and, in truth, I am not much of pudding cook. I made the kitchen table look pretty. I put the blue and white tablecloth on it with the blue and white china, and placed a large bowl of hyacinths in the centre. I filled a small glass candle-stick with a white candle and put it on the mantlepiece over the fireplace. Then I washed my hair and ironed it dry on the ironing board which was not a success. I had read somewhere that curly hair can be straightened by running an iron over it but in my opinion, this is not the case. Certainly the result looked very odd which was upsetting since I wished to look my best, not my worst, which is without any hinderance much more difficult than it was. Throughout the day my state of mind was not as peaceful as I wished it to be. My thoughts, awhirl, ran thus: Am I arranging a seduction scene? A good dinner, and good wine in a comfortable, cosy house with candles and classical music are surely the traditional props to early evening romantic declarations of love and later evening physical demonstrations of the same? "There are so many predatory women about, Victoria," a friend once said to me, "who, desperate, despite all the protestations to the contrary by feminists, seduce men in any devious way they can." Surely I wasn't behaving like that? Or was I? What did I expect Mark to do? And what did Mark expect me to expect? And what did I hope for? Thinking about these questions while I browned the meat, peeled the potatoes and skinned the onions, I decided that women did not KNOW exactly what they expected or hoped for. This is because, I concluded, it would seem too clinical and too contrived to be precise about their expectations. For my part, I simply cannot visualize the sexual act in motion. When I anticipated the evening progressing and I thought of Mark's arms encircling me, his lips kissing me and his hand touching my breast, what might then ensue simply does not appear as a picture in my mind. Somehow it seems to have censored any suggestion of that image. But I can write now, that in reality the sexual act was quite unique. perhaps it was because Mark had, earlier in the evening, declared love. He had fallen in love, he said, the first day he came into the shop and we had talked of daffodils - my fondness for them and his dislike. That I had too fallen in love were sentiments I think he already sensed. "Making love" then tonight, was not a euphemism for "having sex," we made love, uniting ourselves in mind and body. So much is talked about sex, so much written about sex, so much sex is shown in films and on the television but, in spite of all these revelations, all this honesty(?), and all these frank discussions (where imagination has no possible place) the magic of a man and a woman loving each other physically is never, I think, conveyed even minutely. Perhaps it isn't possible to voice, to describe or portray magic, the magic felt by the two persons involved. Possibly it is one of God's jokes that He created us to feel things that are truly indescribable. Nobody, for instance, seems to agree on the concept of happiness or what it is or what it is not. Pain too, is indescribable, and as it is impossible to measure pain it is equally impossible to measure euphoria. But the pure pleasure I felt when Mark and I made love was very much greater than anything I had previously believed possible for myself. I did, in truth, feel shy about taking my clothes off since despite constant dieting, my figure, to say the least, is somewhat less than perfect. But perhaps consistent worry about being thin, getting thin and staying thin is a trifle absurd if your partner loves you and you love him? That is not to say he or she would like you to be fat, but worrying about size, talking about it and thinking about it is not expedient, and I shall try to reduce the time I have previously given to this matter. Another subject that seems to produce endless anxiety in women, and in men for all I know, is the orgasm. That orgasm with a capital O. I knew nothing of female orgasms until the late 60's, when it became the fashion to explore publicly all possibilities and pleasures connected with them. My first knowledge of orgasms was gleaned from reading a woman's magazine during a train journey to Portsmouth. I was astonished at its contents. Naturally for those of us who previously knew nothing of orgasms their appearance was something of a revelation. Suddenly, many women who had no experience of the revealed ecstasy now knew of their deprivation and felt a bit cheated, and disappointed. They felt somewhat angry that their portion of this pleasure was missing in their lives, and not in the least likely to come their way. The magazine then suggested that if you were at a stage in your marriage or partnership where it seemed too late to discuss new excitements for yourself in bed, a vibrator might well come in handy. If, it went on to say, the only conversations that had taken place between you had been about the mortgage, the mother-in-law, or the school fees, then this was the device to answer your sexual needs. I read later that this idea was not successful since most women who might have craved one had absolutely no idea where it could be purchased. Since then, it is said, psychiatrists, psychologists and sex-counsellors, et al, have enriched themselves prodigiously on advising neurotic women on "how to achieve orgasm." But I have no knowledge of how successful they have been, and would be suspicious of any figures given. Orgasms are, surely, a private matter and any discussions of them probably fallacious. I have written enough now. Suffice to say that my cup overflows. I thank God for it and pray that nothing untoward occurs in the future to modify these feelings of joy and love that now overwhelm me.

Sunday 17th March

After breakfast Mark left and I went to Matins in the Cathedral on my own. The sermon this morning concerned love, the text from St John's gospel. I was sad that Mark wasn't there to hear it with me, since it seemed to be pertinent to ourselves. After a short walk by the canal this afternoon, I settled in front of the fire and read Proust, trying to dispel the thousand thoughts of Mark that ran through my mind unceasingly. But I have to admit failure with Proust; I find it unreadable. If I cannot join the ranks of elite who profess that Proust changed their lives, then so be it. I shall, by choice, remain ignorant of its art. It is quite impossible for me to have patience with anyone so self-absorbed, so self-obsessed. He must have been as irritating to his family as Peggie Archer is to hers.

Thursday 21st March

Today Mrs. Pratt was wearing a new dress which did not suit her in the least. The material was bright pink polyester, it was décolleté above the knees, and Mrs. Pratt's knees are not ones that should be exposed to the general public. She told me that she had bought the white high heels and matching handbag in Debenhams Boutique Department, and I believe her. A strange and revolting scent pervaded the shop. It was, Mrs. Pratt revealed, "Luscious to Touch" by Revlon. She then laughed rather hysterically I thought, and she said she hoped that it would prove to be the case. More understanding of this remark, and Mrs. Pratt's general demeanour, came to me when she told me that she would shut the shop at lunchtime today. An old friend, she said, one Terry McGough, and herself were to visit the Wellchester Arms for a drink to discuss the Caravan Clubs' summer outing arrangements. In this instance, unlike the whereabouts of her purchased handbag and shoes, I did NOT believe her. Mark telephoned and sounded worried. He said one of his pupils, a boy by the name of Paul Stoat, had gone missing at lunch time. This evening he had been found in the bicycle shed, drunk. Paul Stoat, is, apparently, a boy with problems. Mark suggested a visit to his Aunt Eliza, who lives in Portsmouth, one weekend in June. His aunt Eliza is a woman of character, he said, and stated that he had a great fondness for her. This weekend he is on duty, but we arranged to meet for dinner next Tuesday. "Thank you, JC," I said as I got into bed, "for myself at the moment all seems to be very well. But perhaps you should keep watch over

Mrs. Pratt. I am under the impression the path of righteousness is not the one she wishes to tread henceforth. I think reading about the vicissitudes of the Royal Family's lives are leading her astray. That is to say she thinks what is good enough for them is good enough for her.

Saturday 23rd March

    I took a bus into Bath to visit Father. I wanted to tell him about Mark and thought, erroneously, that he would be pleased. Well not pleased because father was never positively pleased, but I hoped he would show some interest or at least be pleased for me. But of course it is the truth that people do not change, ever, and Father who had seldom been interested in others, (his full attention and interest only ever focusing on himself) was much keener on discussing the goings-on in Blueberry Rise, and his star-role in them, than my good fortune in meeting Mark. What an egotistical, selfish, boring old sod he is I thought as I nodded and smiled at him. On the bus home I wondered (a) why children are universally expected to love their parents and (b) if they do not, why this is thought so shocking, not only by the people they might tell of it, but more so, by themselves. As a matter of fact I discovered, thinking about father all the way home, that not only do I not love him but that I hate him. "Listen JC.," I said, in the bath, "it is no good whatsoever telling me to love my mother and father as I love myself. It is quite impossible to love such a one as father, and furthermore, I do not forgive him for his insufferable selfishness and his neglect of mother during her life, and of myself during my childhood. He is a monster, and the sole reason I visit him is out of duty. Should he choke on his teeth and die I would not be moved, as they say. Forgive me JC, the cause of my anger is hard to repudiate, to forget, or forgive."

Tuesday 26th March

It was a warm day for March. The polyanthas and primroses were a carpet in the garden.

Mark came to dinner. I made carrot and orange soup and baked lemon sole which we had with mashed potatoes and an endive and watercress salad. I had bought a tolerable bottle of white wine to drink with it. I was pleased with the dinner, and did not find it difficult to cook. I think that cooking and gardening has always daunted me because of the obsessive way women have discussed these subjects over the years. Insinuating that unless I studied the art of cooking and gardening profusely, the plants I planted would not grow and that the sauces I made would curdle, or the meat would burn. It is quite obvious to me now that this is not true, and, if a person can read a recipe book or the instructions on the back of a packet of seeds, cooking is within their grasp and their gardens could look tip-top in no time.

Lovers are never at a loss for conversation primarily I suppose because talking about each other gives them endless scope for enjoyment, in a subject in which they excel. And

Mark and I are no exception to this truth. At about 10.30 I put a Beatles tape on in the kitchen and we danced, and we kissed and made love on a sheepskin rug. We felt merry and young and not guilty or ridiculous for so feeling. The wonder of it all is quite overwhelming.

Being-in-love in middle-age is BRILLIANT as Sarah would say. What difficulties could there be, I wonder?

Friday 29th March

Father Murphy had tea with me this afternoon. His conversation was most disturbing. He said that his FAITH and the PRIESTHOOD and his VOWS were all getting too much for him. He was, after all, a man, he said, a statement which I did not deny. "But nothing has changed, Father Murphy," I said, "you always were a man of sorts." He told me that Molly O'Shea, the Tempting Lady in the Leotard, had continued coming to the coffee mornings, and that she singled him out for conversation. Father Murphy knew well of his talent for conversation and was not, therefore, at all surprised at her preference for him. Father O'Sullivan was not, by any manner of means, a conversationalist, and Father Donaghue spat when he spoke. Father Murphy and Molly O'Shea had a particular interest in common. They both loved butterflies. But, although discussing butterflies with the lady F.M. said his thoughts were elsewhere and he remembered clearly the sight of her naked flesh. "It haunts me at night," he said. Of course I understand Father Murphy's desires particularly now when in the night, alone,

I long for Mark and his image, haunts me. I advised Father Murphy to ask for a short retreat holiday, perhaps to his Mother Country. He was not impressed with this idea and said everyone knew Irish girls were the prettiest in the world and there would be more temptation for him to overcome. "In a monastery in Southern Ireland, Father Murphy," I said, "there will be no girls whatsoever to tempt you." "You don't know the half of it, Missus," he said moodily, and then left no doubt, to drown his sorrows in the Lounge bar of the Wellchester Arms.

Mark telephoned and we talked for an hour. Mostly about us but a minute or two was spent on Paul Stoat. Term ends tomorrow and apparently Paul's trunk, when opened for packing, contained a dead rat. Oddly, the rats head had been cut off. Paul said he thought it was prophetic, but when Mark asked him what he meant, he refused to elaborate.

Monday 1st April

Today Harriet, Tom and Sarah flew to Austria with Leo and Grace, for a ski-ing holiday. I hope there is a dusting of spring snow for them and that the sun shines. I also hope that Grace does NOT make such good fondu as I used to, and, on reflection, I hope the sun doesn't shine every day.

Easter Day 7th April

A lovely, bright day. The Cathedral was very full indeed. I wondered whether the fact that the sun shone made a difference to the attendance. Or do people during Easter week remember that Christ died for us and come to church on Easter Sunday to give thanks to Him? If I was Jesus Christ looking down here I'm not sure I would feel that the whole agonizing business of dying on the cross had been worthwhile at all. Most of the people He saved don't seem in the least grateful. But then difficult as it is to imagine, Christ is all loving and all forgiving, unlike me, so I think He would have thought His life a fair exchange for ours.

Liz, Rodney and Gus were there. Does Gus get paid to go with them to look good, as it were. The Ely family all happily together? I suppose the sight irritates me because I would myself like to be in Church with my family and not there on my own.

Mark and his pupils are coming home from Austria tomorrow, thank God. I have missed him so much it has made me ill. Cleopatra, when Anthony went to Egypt and left her behind, expressed a wish to drink mandragora so that she could "sleep out this great gap of time." I know exactly what she meant; without the man or woman loved, the day and the night seem endless, empty and dreary, and pass by in a state of unreality. I have lost several pounds in weight. The sole consolation for a week's deprivation of Mark.

I had made an Easter cake but it was quite revolting. I scattered it in the garden and the birds seem to like it. It wasn't then a total waste of time and money.

Wednesday 10th April

It was quite euphoric seeing Mark today. His face had burnt brown from ski-ing and he looked very handsome. While we exchanged news it seemed as though my breathe came in gasps, and agitated, somehow I couldn't think clearly. Does this state of being last I wonder, when the pulses race, the heart thumps and beats in the breast and cloudy disorientation descends over the mind rendering it incapable of any efficient, clear and accurate actions or judgements. I have to admit that nothing much of late seems to get done well. Put kindly, my behaviour at the moment is consistently absent-minded, but less kindly, it is thoroughly inept. Perhaps the substance of a relationship is something to be looked forward to so that everyday life can continue in a sensible and responsible way. Of course that last thought does sound very dull but, I suppose, dullness is the real stuff of life.

We went to Mark's flat which is on the ground floor of the main school building. It had a lovely view from the sitting-room and the bedroom. It overlooks the Windwell Valley, which sweeps down to the river Well. A river which winds its way, snakelike, through the lush countryside of Wiltshire and Dorset, meandering, it is said, all the way to Yeovil.

The bathroom was very untidy and the bath looked grey with age and dirty. The bedroom was sparse of furniture, just a single bed, a cupboard and a small chest of drawers. No pretty rugs, or flowers or pictures anywhere, nothing in fact to stamp it as his, in the way a woman stamps her house or her room. I am convinced that men do not notice dirty baths, piles of washing-up, stains on the carpet, stairs littered with debris or anything similar, but, if they do notice they do not care. They think it is of no particular importance, and leave it as it is. I cannot image why it is generally thought that men and women are similarly fashioned in either character or abilities. It is quite clear to me that this is not at all the case and that, in general terms, they have little universally in common except sexual desire, one for the other, and only that, sometimes. This conclusion is neither good or bad, it is simply a statement of fact.

We looked round the school which reminded me of St Anne's, and, indeed, every other public school I have ever visited. Stairs with deep indentations where many feet have trod, a large dining-room with long polished tabletops smelling strongly of furniture polish, and depressing lavatory blocks with graffiti on the back of the doors.

I saw a photograph of Anna and Posy taken two years ago by a Scottish loch. It was difficult to see Posy clearly, but Anna who was wearing hiking boots, a large jersey, and jeans, looked distinctly Greeham Commonish. But I thought she had a pretty face. It seems she has started on a Sociology Course at Exeter College with a view to acquiring a job in the Social Services. After three years reading extensive feminist tracts and such like, she should be in a tip-top position to "find herself" which is the wish she had, and the reason she gave, for leaving Mark when she did. What I always wonder about people who have "found themselves," who have arrived at Shangri-La, as it were, is: what happens next? Where else is there to go if you have arrived in the middle years, and are not, like the rest of us, still on the trail for life's truth?

We had lunch in Marlborough, and as the afternoon was warm and sunny we walked along the Windwell Valley to the village of Collyston Magnus. On our walk Mark told me that Dorothy Wordsworth had no teeth left whatsoever, by the age of thirty. I would myself, I thought, without the wonders of modern science, be dead now instead of enjoying the wonders of life, but I said nothing of this to Mark. Operations are not, in general, a topic to inspire romantic declarations. Later we had supper in Maplewood Road, and made love in the light of the fire's bright flames, and it was all quite literally out-of-this-world-fantasy.

I awoke at 3 o'clock and remembered that in Marlborough I had seen Rodney Ely, with an unknown woman on his arm, leaving the George and Dragon Hotel. How odd I thought as I went back to sleep, which I did almost immediately. Mark, happily, does not snore. I read somewhere that most men do.

Sunday 14th April

I went to Matins at the Cathedral. The collect, for the First Sunday after Easter said something to the effect that we should always service God in Pureness of Living and

Truth as Christ did, putting away the "leaven of malice and wickedness." (I think leaven means corrupt). I mused that the love affair in which I am engrossed with Mark could not be described strictly as Pureness of Living and Truth, but to me, it certainly seems so. It contains no malice, and wickedness, I would say, is relative. For my part, the relationship I have with Mark is pure, and has an innocence of its own.

Monday 15th April

Mrs. Pratt didn't get in until 10.30, and she looked distinctly seedy when she did. She hadn't been sleeping well lately she said, and had therefore taken a sleeping tablet to ensure a good night's repose. "Well, it was certainly effective," I said laughing. Mrs. Pratt for her part, did not laugh then or at any other time during the morning. She started every time the telephone rang and seemed disappointed when it became clear that the caller wished to order flowers. What else would callers wish for when telephoning a flower shop, I asked myself. But it became obvious that Mrs. Pratt was awaiting a call from Someone Else. Someone other than a person wishing to purchase flowers. When I left at one o'clock no call had been received that afforded her any joy, but perhaps this afternoon the anticipated, and promised, I suspect, telephone call will come. Poor Mrs. Pratt. The price in the market place for an affair has always been high, and plus ça change it seems. I thought of the affair I had when I was married to Leo and the agony of it all. And most of all when I discovered the lover as a superlative bastard, romancing simultaneously several other unhappily married ladies living in Brighton. Ah well those tears have all been shed…

**Thursday, Friday, Saturday, Sunday
17th - 21st April**

We went to Portsmouth to stay with Mark's Aunt Eliza, who lives in a small white house high on a hill, overlooking the sea. She was an outrageous, eccentric, magnificent old lady, with bright red hair (dyed) and navy-blue button eyes. When alive, her husband had been an attaché at the Foreign Office, and they had been posted all over the world. God knows what the natives in, for instance, Nigeria, must have thought of Aunt Eliza sweeping about the streets in a long red velvet cloak, the attire apparently she always wore regardless of weather conditions. She regaled us with some astonishing tales. Of intrigues in India, of sailing down rapids in Brazil in leaky boats during tropical rainstorms, and of living for weeks in tents in the Kenyan jungle. There, not only ferocious wild animals, snakes and scorpions were out to get you but, the Mau Mau tribes were also on the move looking for European blood to spill. Aunt Eliza seems to have thrived on it all as only women born in the era of Queen Victoria seem to have done with, I suspect, remarkable courage, enthusiasm and humour. Surely people were much hardier than they are today, and I wonder why that is so. For myself going much further than Bath brings on anxiety symptoms. As for venturing abroad, I simply cannot imagine why anyone should desire such a thing. The noise, the dust, the waiting, the cold or alternatively the heat, the oily food, foreigners trying to sell you things you don't want in the least and are too polite to refuse, loud disco music until 5 a.m. and the three days wait at Gatwick airport, would seem to me a foretaste of hell itself. In any event, Aunt Eliza was still full of energy and ideas to amuse us at the age of 84. On Friday and Saturday we visited a wool church; the small house, now a museum, where Charles Dickens was born and lived with his large family, and the port itself. We saw three of the battleships that had sailed in the fleet to the Falkland Islands War in 1982. I got tired of walking about long before Aunt Eliza, and longed for a rest somewhere in a public place that sold alcoholic refreshment. But it was not to be; we had a temperance day. Aunt Eliza only drinks champagne she told us.

 On Saturday night Mark and I went out alone to the Allingham Theatre in Southampton to see a performance of "The Importance of Being Earnest." The cast was almost universally poor and even made Oscar Wilde's witticisms sound dreary. Query: Do provincial theatres close to become bingo halls for this reason, or other similar? On Sunday morning Aunt Eliza and I went to Matins in her parish church, while Mark read the Sunday newspapers. As always, I wish he had come too. If Mark were a Muslim or a Hindu or whatever I would go to the relevant place of with him, if he so wished. But Mark professes to positive disbelief not negative disbelief and thus feels unable to attend church services without great hypocrisy on his part.

This is for me a definite worry but I shall try not to think about it.

Aunt Eliza was sad to see us leave on Monday afternoon. She is lonely, I think, and although her companion and help, Mrs. Moon, is a good woman and looks after her needs well, Aunt Eliza still enjoys entertaining and in turn being entertained.

We stopped in Winchester on the way home to visit the Cathedral and view Jane Austen's grave. A cold easterly wind blew, and I felt very chilled but Mark seemed unaware of the cold. Perhaps he has a portion of the hardihood that flows in Aunt Eliza's veins, and which very definitely does not flow in mine.

I had a letter from the Inspector of Taxes, and one from my solicitor when I got home. As yet I haven't opened them and shall not do so until I have had at least two gin and tonics. Letters from either of these persons are not welcome.

Wednesday 24th April

Diana Cassington-Mackenzie awoke me with a telephone call at 7.15. Diana is one of those people who exalt in early rising, and feels self-righteous for so doing. Most of us, of course, do not share this enthusiasm, I know I certainly do not. I never fail to feel irritated when the spectacular dawn I have missed by sleeping late, is described to me. Diana inevitably then says, and this morning was no exception: "What a pity you slept through it, for your sake." The reason she telephoned was that she urgently wanted me to know that she had, at a dinner party last week, met a "wonderful man." Yes, he was married but my dear who wasn't ... and of course his marriage was unhappy, but for one reason or another he had to be brave and remain united. They had arranged to meet for lunch next week in a Chelsea Brasserie. "To exchange tales of stale marriages," I asked "Not at all" she said, "quite the contrary. You are not the only one, you know Victoria, who looks to the mind as well as the body of a man. Anyway we are both jolly interested in the opera and I hope we shall discuss my favourite passages in Aida. He knows a lot about Aida." Diana, as far as I know, has never been remotely interested in any kind of music, let alone the opera, but I said nothing of this to her. She sounded cheerful and optimistic and I don't relish the role of censorious friend. I sometimes think I am sanctimonious, and priggish, and she obviously does too. She rang off saying she was going to buy a new dress from Caroline Charles and she would keep me in possession of any relevant information concerning herself and the LOVER. About Mark and myself we had not spoken.

    Father, the matron at Blueberry Rise informed me on the telephone this evening, was impossible. Had he always been so, she inquired. "As long as I can remember," I said, "father has been impossible." Apparently he had peed into Mr. Fentley's slippers, and Mr. Fentley was quite outraged.

Saturday 27th April

Harriet and Sarah arrived from London and Marlborough respectively this morning. It was lovely to see them and catch up on all the news. They seemed, uncharacteristically, to be pleased to see each other too. Is it, I wonder, part of the growing-up process when sisters, (or brothers), previously enjoying no harmonious relationship, and fighting on all counts, suddenly talk and listen to each other courteously instead of contemptuously? The skiing holiday, they said, had been enjoyable. There had been abundant spring snow, the chalet was comfortable and there were not too many people on the slopes. Harriet said Grace was a good skier but, not only could she not cook fondue, she couldn't or wouldn't cook at all, not even the breakfast. The pieces of information passed on about Leo makes me suspect he has not changed in the least but Grace, with quite different needs from mine, does not find him insufferable. Au contraire, she loves him apparently. (I might say in a catty mood, Amazing Grace). Leo, Sarah said, had a large boil on his lip throughout the holiday.

I told them briefly about Mark and said he was coming to supper. They seemed pleased. Pleased they would meet him, and pleased for me. I decided that we would have a boiled chicken cooked with carrots, onions and herbs, and new potatoes (Cyprus), followed by a homemade apple tart. I made it while we were talking. This afternoon we went to see "Out of Africa" during which we wept considerably. Goodness knows why since the white aristocracy in Kenya were, in the 20's and 30's it is said, unspeakable. I think and hope supper and the meeting between Mark and the girls was a success. I felt somewhat nervous and probably drank too much as a result. Much talk took place but about what is a little unclear in my mind. I know Sarah spoke of her A-Level English Course and discussed with Mark the difficulties of understanding the language of Chaucer. He said he would help her should the occasion arise. Harriet asked him about Tuscany since she is anxious to holiday there one summer. I remember he told her of the olive groves, the ubiquitous soldier-like Cypress trees, and the wild flowers. He spoke of Florence, and of Pisa, I remember.

 I had asked Mark not to stay in Maplewood Road tonight, the children's first night of meeting him. I am convinced it is difficult for children to accustom themselves to their parent's new affiliations. Many different feelings will overcome them and their reactions to the newcomer will be ambiguous. But I suppose the most difficult concept of all is to imagine their mother or father, in bed with someone else - the idea being either ridiculous or revolting, or both.

 I am writing this in bed. It is past midnight. The clock in St Peter's Church has just chimed twelve times. I thought of Mark and how funny and kind and lovely he was. And I thought of Harriet and Sarah and how they had been lively and merry tonight. I felt proud of my daughters, and I love them both dearly.

 The patchwork in my eiderdown is, I see, falling to pieces. I shall have to mend it tomorrow.

Monday 29th April

Wellchester School for Boys started the Summer Term today. Will there be much cricket to watch, to talk about, to play in, for Mark, I wonder. I know nothing whatsoever of cricket. Tom played tennis.

Wednesday 1st May

Mrs. Pratt hummed untunefully several bars of "I did it my way" in the shop this morning. "Old blue eyes knew a thing or two" she said. She went on to say that she was very glad to read in the Sun Newspaper that Princess Anne was now the most popular young Royal. She deserves it, she pointed out to me, the Princess works very hard for Save the Children, and keeps her nose clean. Quite so, I thought. I ventured to ask Mrs. Pratt whether her meeting with Terry McGough in the Wellchester Arms, to arrange the Summer Party for the Caravan Club, had been successful. It had been, apparently, in more ways than one. She added that "to be perfectly honest they were meeting again today to tie-up some ends." She would therefore be leaving the shop at one o'clock sharp. If Mr. Pratt called this morning she was not going to mention her lunchtime rendezvous since she said she was minded to keep all arrangements for the Party a secret, a surprise for him, as it were. Quite so, I thought for the second time this morning. Mrs. Pratt, who is 53, was wearing a short leather skirt, and high heeled black suede shoes.

Guy Bell rang and asked me out to dinner on Friday night. I had completely forgotten of his existence and said, untruthfully, that on Friday night, I was going to the cinema with Liz Ely. Not to worry he would ring again soon, he said. I shall have to tell him my single status has changed and that, in a manner of speaking, I am no longer free.

Saturday 4th May

Mark drove me to Bath to visit father who was at his very worst. He took out his teeth when he was talking to Mark and put them on a copy of a Harold Robbins novel which was prominently placed on the bedside table. I am sure he did it on purpose to embarrass me - in which case he did well. When told Mark was a teacher, father said as far as he was concerned all teachers, nowadays, were communists who encouraged the young not in the pursuit of knowledge but in the pursuit of sex, violence and bad language. This was a certain fact he said and not to be disputed. Mark did not dispute it as I had told him that disputing anything with one Percy Troubridge was a complete waste of time. He is, in his eyes, omniscient. As a result of this erroneous opinion on his part I remember very dull monotones during my childhood, mother and I his unwilling, but captive and silent audience. Mark agreed, while we were dining in Bath, that father was intolerable but insisted that at his age he wouldn't change and that I should accept him as he was. I tried to explain to Mark how hatred is impossible to eliminate, like dry rot or damp rot its poison seeps everywhere. "To exterminate the hatred it would be necessary to exterminate me," I said. I think Mark thought that two gins and tonics before dinner were, perhaps, two too many and the passion I felt was the result of an excess. I knew, of course, that it was no such thing. Anyone, I think, who has had real cause in childhood to feel anger at the selfish and cruel behaviour of their parents, in whatever form, knows that the wounds ever continue to bleed. Anyway since Mark's parents were very happy in their married life it was unlikely that he would ever understand even a little of my feelings, so I asked him why A-Level English Literature never included works of Mrs. Gaskell. As a matter of fact I did not know if this was at all true, and I expect A-Level English Literature has included her works, but it changed the subject, and my passion spent I needed a safe subject to discuss.

Mark, on duty tomorrow dropped me home at half past ten. I made a cup of tea and listened to evocative, soothing Beethoven's 5th violin concerto. Query: when do I not, when I want to think? My thoughts ran thus: men and women are able only, in part, to understand one another. There is a point arrived at when, whatever words are used by either, and whatever is said, is quite incomprehensible to the other party; like listening to some-one talking an unknown foreign language. When this point is reached, I think the subject should be changed. The batteries in my radio gave up at this moment of my reverie and I went to bed with a flakey bar and a copy of "Larkrise to Candleford." I love this book except I think keeping a pig throughout the year as a friend, and then killing it at Christmas, seems the ultimate betrayal.

Sunday 5th May

For a reason unknown to myself, I felt dispirited in the Cathedral this morning. The interior of this building looked lovely, with bowls of bluebells and primroses placed on the stone shelves alongside the pews. And pots of green leaves and large white daises were dotted about, here and there. Shafts of pale spring sunlight shone through the beautiful Norman stained-glass windows, and a wood pigeon cooed outside in the Close. So what was wrong with me? Why did I feel like weeping when we sang, inexplicably, since non-one was getting married, "0 Perfect Love, all human thought transcending." Perhaps the idea of Perfect Love is too much or too ridiculous to contemplate. How many people do I know, for instance, who receive love of any kind, not least the kind they want or need, let alone Perfect Love? I thought of Rodney Ely, obviously about to embark on an extra-marital affair, Mrs. Pratt embarked already it seemed, and Father Murphy wrestling with his conscience and almost admitting to failure. What kind of love were these diverse people expecting or experiencing? I do not know what love it is, but Perfect Love it is not. And mine, with Mark? What kind of love is ours? Why does the importance I attach to the Love of God matter so much to me, that I feel an important part of myself is unknown and perhaps unwanted by Mark? Goodness me, it is difficult to make sense of it all.

If great and wise men and women such as Aristotle, Virgil, Kant, Dr Johnson, Voltaire, Clare Raynor et al, can only point in the right direction, what chance have the rest of us got?

Bucket the dog, and I walked up Wellchester High Street this afternoon. We looked in the shop windows and I decided that everything on display looked much more inviting on a Sunday than on a weekday. Query: Is the old chestnut about that which is unobtainable having more attraction than that which is easily obtained, applicable universally? That is to say do kettles, hoovers, electrical appliances, Indian scarves, bright pink skirts in polyester, or whatever, acquire more allure (as in people) when we can see their attractions but know, irrevocably that immediate possession is impossible?

Tuesday 7th May

Father Murphy had afternoon tea with me today. He looked careworn and seedy, and a little paler and a little thinner than he did two weeks ago. "I'm in a terrible way, Missus" he said, "I can't eat properly, I can't sleep properly, and I can't even pray properly anymore." He stayed for over an hour, rambling on, repeating himself, mentioning Molly O'Shea, cursing a bit and even crying a bit. I comforted him, and made two pots of tea in which I put a little whisky, and a spoonful or two of clover honey. Up until now he has not succumbed to his desire for excitement and penetration of the flesh but it is obviously a great struggle, one I suspect he will not win. He is, of course, in love or in lust, and as I now know moral principles and values get distorted in this singular state of being. I kissed Father Murphy's whiskery cheek as he left and although he seemed surprised, I think he was pleased.

Saturday 11th May

Mark had the whole day off. Last week he discovered that I played tennis, and had booked a court at the Recreation Centre in Canterbury Road. We played three sets and I discovered that I could not play tennis. He beat me 6-0, 6-1, 6-2. How is it my memory is such an untrustworthy chronicler? It distinctly showed me pictures in my mind of myself playing, admittedly twenty years ago, a fine game of tennis. In this imaginary scene I am running smartly about hitting the ball with a good forehand drive and performing well enough, when required, with the backhand. Obviously, I had told Mark about my ability on the court and he had believed me, as indeed I had myself believed this to be so. But it was not so. My tennis performance was terrible. I suppose that either I never was any good at tennis or memory distorts the truth. Mark however said nothing about my poor performance and neither did I.

For lunch we took a picnic to the Windwell Valley. It consisted of: duck pate, French bread and butter, cold sausages, and homemade mayonnaise, boiled eggs, cheddar cheese and two conference pears. I took a tin of Sainsbury's French white wine, and Mark had a tin of Carlsberg. We ate it under an oak tree. After the tennis, the walk and wine I fell asleep with Mark holding my hand.

Walking back to the car, later, Mark talked of Paul Stoat. Paul Stoat was an enigma, he said. He had returned after the holidays with a locked tin box which he, despite being told not to, kept on the end of his bed. Boxes on beds in boarding schools are not allowed, and Mark, as his housemaster, would have to confiscate it. Boarding schools, for those people, male or female, who do not wish to be part of a group, one of the boys, in the school team or whatever, are a terrible experience never forgotten. Those who prefer a more solitary existence than can ever be found in community life, find community life of any description, unendurable. I know because I am one of them. Paul Stoat is, I suspect, one of them too. I pity him.

Mark said as went upstairs tonight that he had been wanting to make love to me all day and, that he hoped I was ready for a long night. I told him not to boast, "Remember we are middle-aged," I said. As it turned out, he wasn't boasting.

Sunday 12th May

I did not go to the Cathedral this morning. The mood I was in caught from the sins of the flesh was not conducive to repentance or virtue or hymn singing. Mark left after breakfast and I went back to bed. I played my favourite tapes of the early Beatles. Mark says my icon of Jesus Christ is a John Lennon lookalike and, in all probability, the main reason for my Christian passion. I said nonsense, but on the contrary, the reason I like John Lennon was because he looks like Jesus Christ. Each individual's view of life, I suppose, simply depends on how he views it. As William Blake said: As a man is, so he sees.

I found a letter this evening I had had from Peter Mallet, the BORE. I wonder whether he has found a suitable someone, someone in any event, more suitable than me. I do hope so.

Monday 13th May

Liz Ely and I had lunch in Poppy's Tea Room. She said judging by the amount of work she had to do in the library people must still be reading books, although God knows, she saw no evidence of it in her house. Rodney watched the television every night (when he wasn't going to Masons meetings which he did more often these days) and Gus, when he was in, did likewise. She said that Gus had mentioned, in a casual way, that Sarah was thinking of accompanying him to India this summer. As she can barely afford the fare to Wellchester from Marlborough more than once a month, how she would pay her passage to India, as it were, is an interesting thought. Liz said she didn't like talking about money and where Sarah got hers from was, frankly, none of her business. Liz frequently hints that she suspects that I am much richer than I appear to be and that I merely pretend to be poor for absurd reasons, such as inverted snobbery or a "real desire to be one of the people."

She can, of course, think whatever she pleases, discussing money is the subject I dislike most and have no wish to pursue. While we queued to pay for our lunch Liz said Rodney's office was sending him on a Training Weekend at the end of July. She said it was the first course he had ever been on and he was, she thought, looking forward to it, even strangely excited by the idea. Quite so.

Friday 17th May

Mrs. Pratt and I spent all day in St Michael's and All Angels, the Parish Church of Mereton Ogmore, arranging flowers. A wedding was to take place there on the following day between two members of the Caravan Touring Club, one David Crisp to one Linda Morris. Mrs. Pratt obviously did not regard the church as a sacred place, a place of sanctity or reverence. I noticed she did not feel the need to whisper or even lower her voice and had no interest whatsoever in the belfry tower, the Norman arches, or the lancet windows. No, she might have been in the bingo hall, or at the Caravan Touring Social Club, and probably imagined she was. She lit a cigarette in the porch and then shouted instructions at me down the centre aisle. The flower arrangements, when finished, looked dreadful, I thought. Mrs. Pratt's premise that there is safety in numbers obviously applied to wedding flowers and every single crevice available she filled with an arrangement of one sort or another. For my part I hate those arrangements; the poor flowers contorted into strange, unnatural positions. I have noticed that shortly after being thus "arranged" they often die.

At lunchtime I walked round the church yard. It was full of old, tottering, grimy gravestones, the wording on the stone slabs lost with time and the English weather. I did decipher one name: Harriet Wodehouse, who apparently died in 1837 aged 23 "a dearly beloved wife and mother." "Where are you now, Harriet Wodehouse, where are you now?" I asked out loud. And where indeed are all the other souls departed from this life, whose bones have slowly turned to dust in those graves, in that English Churchyard? I must remember to ask JC for some pointers to this recurrent question of departing souls' destination. I have in fact asked him before but I have had no satisfactory answer. I spotted amongst the unkempt grass of St Michael's and All Angels churchyard, two plastic cups, about seven toffee papers, two Sainsbury's carrier bags, and what appeared to be a used condom. A little different from the images conjured up by Grey's country churchyard, I thought to myself.

Later when I was sweeping up in the vestry, I recalled my own wedding day with Leo Scott. What a grand occasion it had been, with all the material trappings of happiness money could buy. It was only the riches of the soul and spiritual union that were absent.

I listened to the Archers at supper. Why I wonder is Brian Aldridge turning into a sex maniac? A 1985 version of Tom Jones, the rollicking, racy, crude and sexy squire? The people responsible for writing the Archers should realize that the followers of Ambridge's intrigues do NOT wish to have the unpleasantness's of life thrust upon them in this series. Reading a newspaper is all we need to do to appreciate life's unending miseries. Ambridge, I feel, should be a place of refuge. I need the Archers to soothe me, not to distress me. It is for me a dream village that is almost possible to imagine, and in which I can almost believe, and I wish it to stay that way, forever.

Saturday and Sunday 24th and 25th May

Mark had the weekend off and on Saturday afternoon we drove to Stratford-on-Avon. We had booked tickets for a performance of Julius Caesar, my favourite Shakespeare play (in fact I only know four). Simply reading or hearing the words of this play makes me weep; lines such as: If I could pray to move, prayers would move me, But I am constant as the Northern Star... or: If you have tears, prepare to shed them now... or: He was my friend, faithful and just to me... and the most touching of all:
and the elements
so mixed in him that Nature might stand up
and say to all the world, "This was a man".

After the performance Mark took my hand, and we walked slowly back to Hillcrest Bed and Breakfast where we were staying the night. In bed we discussed aspects of friendship, its limits and lengths until the early hours. Caesar might well have been wary of friendship if Anthony, Brutus and Casius were supposed to be his best friends. With friends like those who needs enemies, he might have thought to himself, had he been as familiar with cliches as Mrs. Pratt.

Later we made love passionately, the sweet sound of the Avon murmuring its way down river and with a fresh southerly wind blowing in through the open window. Next morning after a delicious breakfast of eggs and bacon, toast and marmalade, orange juice and many cups of tea, we walked round Stratford. Stratford itself was enormously unpleasant, overflowing with tourists who spewed out of buses in large, inseparable groups. Sartre who maintained that hell was other people, a sentiment I agree with in part, would not have liked it at all in Stratford today. Nor did we. We drove south into the Cotswolds and stopped at The Queen's Arms, Bibury, for lunch. In the carpark before we left for Wellchester, Mark kissed me and I felt exquisitely happy. With the truly loved one, a carpark is just as romantic as a moonlit balcony overlooking a bay, or wherever romance is thought to be at its best. For my part I could kiss Mark right beside the dustbin shed, or even in it, and the magic would still be there.

Wednesday 29th May

Diana rang. She said her man was "quite divine." He understood her, she said, as no man had ever done before and, of course, she was the first woman he had ever met who seemed to understand him so completely - sympathizing with his needs, and forgiving his past transgressions, neither of which his wife seemed capable of doing. Diana then talked at great speed for ten minutes about: the man, and the WONDER of him. He was good-looking, tall, rich, intelligent, and, HE WAS A GREAT LOVER. God everything was bliss, she said. Henry was going fishing in Scotland in July. She hoped she and THE MAN would be able to hop over to Le Touquet for a night or two and play exciting games at the casino, and with each other. The man had mentioned that for himself black underclothes were a BIG TURN ON and Diana, ever anxious to please, was off to Harrods to purchase black silk bras and pants. "I do hope your affair with, I've forgotten-his-name, is going well Victoria," she said as she rang off. Had she not rung off I could have told her that I am not having an affair. I am in love and building a relationship which, in my opinion, is something quite else, something quite different altogether.

Monday 3rd June

Today there was a bus strike. I walked to work which was lovely and I cannot imagine why I don't do it more often. Hurrying down the streets I peeped into the front gardens full of June colours. I saw honeysuckles, seringas, pinks and poppies and of course an abundance of traditional roses, dog roses and wild roses. House Martins swooped about feeding their young, nesting in the eaves, some coming very close to my head - too close. Whilst I love the beauty of birds, and am entranced by their song, if a wild bird and myself were in a room together I do not know who would die of fright first, the bird or me. I cannot understand this fear in myself at all, rationally it seems completely absurd to fear a small, frightened bird, but I do. Perhaps it is a primeval fear and mine is a primitive reaction. Who knows?

    Mrs. Pratt asked me to look after the shop all day for her next Wednesday. She is going to watch Ascot on the television. Her friend from the Caravan Touring Club, Mrs. Bradley, is to spend the day with her, for the company, she said. I suspect numerous glasses of Bristol Cream Dry Sherry will be drunk and several packets of Players No 1 will be smoked over intense discussions about, the Royal Family. Their clothes, their habits, their weight, how much they eat and drink, quarrel, and how often they make love. All this is rich food for speculators such as Mrs. Pratt and Mrs. Bradley. Plenty of range there for imagination to run amok. I hope Mrs. Bradley can give more satisfactory answers than I, to questions asked. Since Mrs. Pratt holds her in high regard, I expect she can. Gladly I told Mrs. Pratt I would look after the shop while she took the day off. The shop is very pleasing in Mrs. Pratt's absence.

    Tom rang, He wants to stay on the night of Saturday 8th. He will arrive sometime, he said, but was not at all sure whether it would be before lunch, after lunch, before dinner or for late dinner. Do the younger generation make these flexible plans with each other, as they do with their parents, I wonder? I can visualize none of them actually ever meeting with the amount of indecision and ifs, and buts, that accompanies any question of time precision.

    I danced by myself in the kitchen tonight to the rhythms of a South American Band, drank two or three glasses of wine, and I SMOKED a Gauloise cigarette Mark had left here (it was wonderful) and felt generally well pleased and young. However, when I got into bed my glasses were elsewhere. Reading was not a possibility and I felt my age, and the feelings of youth deserted me.

Thursday 6th June

Today I felt fat. Measuring myself, I found this to be an actuality not an assumption. I think the way fat creeps up silently upon one is extraordinarily unfair. By simply relaxing self-imposed rules for even a day or two, buttons cease to do up and the flat stomach wished for and fought for, once again looks like a blown-up balloon. Eating is one factor of life necessary for existence and, planning how to exist without gaining weight, seems a never-ending struggle, you versus you, as it were. I'll try cutting down the Mars Bars. Father Murphy rang to ask me to meet him in the Lounge Bar of the Wellchester Arms on Friday 14th at 7 o'clock. He sounded upset, and I agreed to meet him. Has he finally tasted the forbidden fruit, I wonder, or does he need further support to strengthen his resolve not to weaken? "JC" I prayed from the bath where I was thinking about it, "could you please help Father Murphy a bit. Temptation for us all, especially when passion runs high, is as You know, difficult to resist. I'm sure the Devil is at his side, the very place where You should be."

Saturday 8th June

I took the early bus down to the market to buy fresh fish and vegetables for supper. It was a sunny day with a slight wind blowing and Wellchester itself looked very beautiful. Walking home I thought about Tom meeting Mark. Tom is at 18, going through the dreaded phase of knowing everything. I can't remember who said: I'm not young enough to know everything ... but whoever it was knew if not everything, a thing or two. Mark came here after lunch and we drove to Bridmouth, a small village in the Windwell Valley. Mark was tired. He said the summer term with A-Level examinations approaching was always stressful with anxious students needing constant help and re-assurance. Sarah, I thought, will need some of it next year. We walked by the river's bank and then lay down in the long grass. Mark fell asleep, and I thought how vulnerable he looked, like a small child. And I thought once again how much I loved him and of how fortunate I was to have fallen-in-love at my age.

Tom arrived shortly after six o'clock with all his dirty washing and a considerable quantity of Cathy's. This he left on the kitchen table in bulging plastic bags. Viewing the books he left on the floor he seems to be studying Nietzsche and Wittgenstein for his philosophy degree, and Jackie Collins, (for a degree of philosophy perhaps). The fish I cooked for supper was delicious, but conversation did not flow and I felt the atmosphere strained. I am not sure that Tom liked Mark, or that Mark liked Tom. They are of course the antithesis one to another. Mark being quiet, reflective and gentle whereas Tom is noisy, and somewhat abrasive.

Mark stayed the night here and it was blissful. I thought Tom could cope with knowing of this arrangement better than the girls but perhaps I am wrong. If my theory about mothers and sons is correct, that the relationship could be a sexual one of sorts, then perhaps he was more affected than the girls would have been. But I haven't read Freud so I would not know. I went to sleep wondering if Mark minded me wearing glasses as much as I mind wearing them, and consoled myself with the thought that perhaps he doesn't notice.

Sunday 9th June

I said I would do Tom's washing and ironing if he come to the Cathedral with me this morning. He came. We left Mark at breakfast saying what a terrible newspaper the Sunday Times had become. Rodney and Liz were at the service, but no Gus. He had gone to a pop festival in Glastonbury they said and not by himself either, insinuating, I thought, that Sarah had gone with him. Sarah is not allowed out of college for the night without my permission and this she had not sought for this weekend. Well, I hope they are wrong. Drugs, drink and fights float before my eyes at the thought of a pop festival, to say nothing of sexual activities I am conversant with, and goodness knows of the ones I am not.

Mark, with much work to do, went straight back to school after lunch. Tom and I sat in the garden and talked until teatime, after which, he drove back to Brighton. He told me that Grace was very spoilt and that her mother, Daphne, quite often stayed with them. Leo apparently couldn't bear Daphne, and Daphne, in her turn, couldn't bear Leo. This made living there less than harmonious, although Tom thought Leo and Grace were well suited. Tom said Cathy liked Grace and when this piece of information seemed to upset me, he said he thought I was suffering from the menopause. He knows all about the menopause he said, which, in actual fact, is more than I do. About Mark, he said nothing.

Thursday 13th June

Mrs. Pratt was quite orgiastic this morning. She and Mrs. Bradley had had a tip-top time watching Ascot yesterday, she said. She had new views on the Royals, none of which I can remember, except she thought Princess Diana looked very sad. "She is not a happy woman, make no mistake," said Mrs. Pratt. I must say, for my part, I would rather be an assistant in Woolworth's electrical department than be Princess Diana. Perhaps she would too now she has found out that with all the wealth in the world, with all the adulation and all the flattery she receives, without a loving relationship it is all as to dust.

Mrs. Pratt I noticed had lost weight. Throughout the morning she hummed her favourite tunes, over and over and over again. "Every time I say Goodbye" obviously evokes happy memories. Every time she hummed it, into her face came a look which she probably imagined to be romantic. In actual fact, she only succeeded in looking grotesque with her small brightly coloured mouth, twisted into a leer. I mentioned her weight loss and she said exercise, or at least the exercise she was currently indulging in, was a great reducer. She was, I suppose, referring to her couplings with Terry McGough which were obviously now taking place at frequent intervals. I said to Mrs. Pratt that I wasn't aware that she liked, or participated in, any form of exercise. She replied, predictably, "to be quite truthful we live and learn all the time in life, I always say." Of that truth, certainly, I agree with her.

Mark telephoned to say that there was a measles epidemic at school. Since I haven't had measles I will not be able to see him for the three weeks quarantine time. O Dear Lord, how will I manage?

Friday 14th June

I met Father Murphy, as arranged, in the Lounge Bar of the Wellchester Arms. His virginity, the subject on which he wished to talk, is still in his possession but only just. He asked me whether I thought he should confess his worldly desires to another Priest, but not in the Confessional. It wasn't enough, he said, to confess his sins and have them absolved by saying the rosary a thousand times, or whatever punishment was metered out to those in the fatherhood harbouring lustful thoughts. No, Father Murphy wanted advice and was at a loss to know who to turn to. His fellow priests being he thought as unworldly as he was himself. I bought him a large whisky and soda and had a double gin and tonic myself, "with ice and a twist of lemon," as they say in novels. I think the gist of what I said to F.M. was that in himself I was sure he knew what was right and what was wrong. For my part, I have found, contrary to what psychiatrists tell their clients, we need a conscience as a guide for the correct way to conduct our lives. It is very simple. If our conscience tells us our behaviour is wrong, then it is wrong. For Father Murphy to ask another what he should do was not necessary, since he, himself, knew quite well. We had another drink or two and became a little merry, well, a bit drunk, in other words. I don't think, ultimately, that we concluded any particular plan of action to pursue. But I do remember saying as we said goodnight that since faith, it is said, moved mountains, I thought his faith could probably manage to keep his trousers round his waist, where they belonged. Father Murphy thought this idea very droll, and laughed and laughed. "JC" I said getting into bed, "You have, up to date, done fuck-all to help Father Murphy. It is simply not good enough" and I turned out the light. At 3.20a.m. I was sick.

Saturday 22nd June

With a headache and hangover I went to Bath to shop and to visit father. Mark's parents are coming to England in

August and I need some new clothes. I love the shops in Bath as I hate them in Wellchester. Even I, with little sense of fashion and no taste, know that Wellchester's answer to Laura Ashley, as in Jill's Fashion Focus or Belinda's Boutique are perfectly dreadful, selling unwearable garments by almost anyone's standards.

To get the unpleasant part of the day over first I visited father as soon as I arrived. Matron was away and a lady, one Mrs. Fig was temporarily in charge of Blueberry Rise. She said Father had been sulking all the week because he wasn't allowed to watch the film of his choice last Sunday night. It had been generally voted by the other residents that an Agatha Christie film was preferable to an Ingmar Bergman. Father had not agreed. He liked Ingmar Bergman's gloomy films. Mrs. Fig said that she found, when dealing with difficult patients, ignoring them was the best policy and had applied this strategy to father. For father this must have been punishment indeed, being ignored would not suit him in the least bit. However, for once, he seemed quite pleased to see me, or in truth, he was pleased with the half bottle of Haig's Scotch whisky I took him. He said it was permitted, but I am not absolutely clear about the rules for alcohol in Blueberry Rise. Father, of course, was never law abiding if the law and himself were not in accord. I hope he doesn't get drunk and lunge out at Mr. Fentley or rape the nurse, Mrs. Hill. (Query: Is rape possible at 76, I wonder).

My clothes quest was disappointing. Either everyone in Bath is very thin or, and I have a feeling this is the truth, I am too fat for the elegant and fashionable clothes on sale. The fact that I don't like fashionable or elegant clothes is probably because I look so ludicrous in them. I simply do not have the figure, or face, to wear them. Instead I shall continue to wear Indian shawls, skirts and boots, long jerseys and cardigans, all the clothes I have always loved to wear. The children consider them much dated and make pointed remarks about "middle aged hippies." I know Harriet would like me to wear more conservative clothes. Her friend's parents wear suits from Jaguar, with lots of gold jewellery and Gucci shoes with gold chains. Their uniform, I suppose, but certainly not mine. Even to oblige Harriet I couldn't do it.

 I came back home with a jar of clover honey I could have bought in Wellchester High Street. As the headache was still thumping about in my head I went to bed early, and wishing for its rapid departure, I took two aspirins.

Sunday 23rd June

 Liz, Rodney, Gus and Sarah and I had lunch in The Black Bear Inn, Mereton Ogmore. Sarah rang early saying she was coming to Wellchester for the day to see Gus, and me. I suggested we all had lunch together and she agreed. It could be fun, she said. It was. Rodney was wearing his jeans jacket, and had combed his thinning hair up and over the bald patch. I do not know why balding men do this since it looks unconvincing and being bald is not, in itself, a detraction. At least I do not think so. Liz was cheerful and talkative especially after her third glass of gin and lime and Gus, bearded now, grunted less than usual, and smiled and spoke a bit more. Sarah, happy it seemed, was wearing silver dungarees and a black T-shirt with a portrait of Karl Marx depicted on the front.

I came home by myself. Sarah and Gus were going to meet some friends, or at least that is what they said they were going to do. I am not quite clear about their relationship. It is difficult to tell nowadays with so little outward show of affection between couples. Being "just friends" could be just that. Anyway I read Jane Austen's "Persuasion" this evening. In this book there is no such difficulty. Understanding, ultimately, who loves who and what is what is totally, thank goodness, comprehensible.

Mark telephoned. We talked for an hour or more. The telephone is no longer a function but a pleasure. I understand now why the children run up such large bills, the joy of talking to a lover is immeasurable.

Tuesday 25th June

It is 2.30p.m. There is silence in the streets. The shops are deserted. It feels like Boxing Day and the ten dreadful days after Christmas. Why is this so? Because everyone, except me, is watching Wimbledon. I know tennis is a game of great skill, but for my part, nothing is more boring to watch than a bloody tennis ball, hopping over and over a net.

Thursday 27th June

I re-applied "Beautiful Black" hair preparation this afternoon. Hair which grows round the temples seems the most resilient to dye. It appears suddenly before one, white. White hair like fat creeps up and takes one unawares, almost overnight. Query: will I have to go on dying my hair black for the next twenty years at 3 weekly intervals. Or. can I grow old gracefully and wear my hair as a white cottage loaf and resemble the Railway Children's mother. An image Harriet always liked and secretly, I think, wished I had resembled more in her teenage years.

The parcel post service brought me a sack of wild flower seeds I had ordered from a catalogue. Needless to say it looked nothing like the Cottage Garden Bag advertised. After two years on my own I am still a gullible fool, and easily duped, and although I like to think of myself as thoroughly "street-wise" (Sarah's word), I am not. In any event I scattered them all over the garden and hope I shall have a profusion of Canterbury Bells, Cornflower and Poppies blooming during the summer months, next year. I will not over-do the hoping as I know hope's limitations but, perhaps, with a little luck, the odd prayer and an early spring, one or two of them will survive and bring me great pleasure in so doing.

Saturday 29th June

Seeing Mark today after three solitary weeks was a wonder, quite breathtaking. In literal terms, I found it hard to breathe let alone speak, and as we hugged and kissed each other as if we could never stop, I felt dizzy, sick and unbalanced on my feet. If the earth ever was to move (and that seems to be the crucial question for relationships in the 80's) for me it did so then, metaphorically speaking, and it was miraculous. Perhaps, on reflection, the earth should only move for people under the age of thirty, to be quite sure of no health risks. With cigarettes, alcohol, chocolate, and all the rest, to tempt us, and then to kill us by so doing, we need no further risks in middle age to cut us down before our allotted span. For my part, therefore, I would prefer the earth to stay where it is. The whole lovely day went by in a blur. I know we laughed hugely, talked intensely, walked a little, gazed in wonder at each other, gossiped, touched and kissed, and made love anywhere and everywhere, blissfully, euphorically. It was a day out of time, which I would like to be able to re-create, whenever I wanted to, throughout my life. To recreate it, as Proust did, so that it lives again as intensely as it did for me today whenever I conjure it up in my mind.

Diana Cassington Mackenzie is coming to lunch tomorrow. Diana likes traditional Sunday lunch, with roast beef and Yorkshire pudding, followed by apple tart, as of yesteryear.

Sunday 30th June

I went to the Cathedral. Alone. Again. The sermon was a text from St Matthew Ch. 7, about "a wise man who built his house upon a rock." Sound advice indeed and particularly easy to follow the reasoning for building just so. The difficulty is, as I see it, that building anything metaphorically analogous to rocks requires time, and patience, and love. Three things which most people today do not possess or wish to know about. Less wise men building not on rocks, but on sand, shoddily, seem to be the main building trade of the 80's. Query: why then are we aghast that many modern houses crack, leak, split, are deserted and then demolished, leaving empty, scarred black holes, when built thus?

Diana came to lunch looking rather wonderful. She was wearing a short black skirt, black stockings, a tight white cashmere jersey, and black high-heeled boots. Mark, I think, was quite astonished at her appearance. Women such as Diana had not, I suspect, come his way before. Conversation was mellifluous since Diana provided it, unceasingly. She asked questions and produced the answers herself, laughed at her own jokes and enjoyed a centre-stage position. The position life she knew had allotted her. At lunch, she ate heartily of the beef and had two helpings of Yorkshire pudding. She asked Mark about Wellchester School, but, in the same breath informed him about her son Hugh's school, Matchams House, a very superior place apparently. "And" said Diana "with children from proper backgrounds, people we all know." Quite. She hurried off to London at 4.30 in her Volkswagen Golf and Mark and I, exhausted, read the Sunday newspapers. Later we discussed Mark's parents' visit to England. They were to stay with Aunt Eliza for the last two weeks of August, and during that time we agreed to arrange a visit there ourselves. Aunt Eliza would be in her element. Four people to boss about would be a real treat for her.

Mark said he thought Diana was "lively" but for his part after any length of time with her he would feel like running away into the hills for solitude, peace, but most of all, silence.

Tuesday 9th July

The telephone was ringing as I got home from the shop at lunchtime. It was Mark. Mark very upset. Today, after breakfast on the last day of term, Paul Stoat's body had been found floating in the River Well. The police had come to the school, he said, but it was thought, in general, that Paul had committed suicide. The sealed box in Mark's possession had been opened. Apparently it contained a letter from his mother explaining why she felt justified leaving his father, and why she was applying for a divorce. His mother's diamond necklace, thought stolen in the holidays, was also in the box. Mark had already spoken to Mrs. Stoat on the telephone, who was quite dumbfounded and unable to take it all in. However, she would come to fetch Paul's belongings when she had contacted his father, she said. Mr. Stoat, since their separation, lived in The Channel Islands. I comforted

Mark as best I could. He sounded very distressed and kept repeating "why didn't Paul speak to me, his housemaster, if he was unhappy?" Well, why indeed? Shouldn't we all listen to our children more. Do I listen to Harriet, Tom and Sarah when they need me and does Mark listen to Posy when she needs him? I wonder. Perhaps Paul thought Mark was too busy to bother, and his parents too pre-occupied with their own lives to have time to listen to whatever it was that drove him to drown himself, if that is what he did. I pondered whether it was something to do with the dead rat in his trunk last term. Someone in the school was obviously bullying him - or was it because he had no friends or because his mother told him about the impending divorce? Or what? The truth is that God alone knows and the rest of us never shall. "JC" I said, in bed, "Please look after Paul wherever he is, because it seems to me that we all failed him here when he needed us."

Saturday 13th July

Paul Stoat's funeral took place today at 2 o'clock in the Parish Church of St Michael's and All Angels, Mereton Ogmore. The coffin, carried down the aisle by four large men, looked very small, and boasted only a single wreath on its lid. There were not more than fifteen people at the ceremony. Mr. and Mrs. Stoat, a few relations, and some members of staff from Wellchester School, including Mr. Ashburton, the headmaster. Mark looked serious and distressed, and was wearing uncharacteristically a grey suit, shirt and tie. I hardly recognized him when we met outside the church. It was the first time I had been in a church with him but the occasion was hardly heartwarming, and the closeness I imagined that could exist during a religious service of any kind, between two people who love each other, was definitely absent. I felt cold and wept for Paul, and probably self-pityingly, for myself and for all mankind in its suffering, and stupidity, and selfishness. Later in the churchyard I read the card that had been attached to the wreath on the top of the coffin. It said: To darling Paul, we are sorry we failed you and that when you spoke we didn't hear. Please forgive us, Mum and Dad.

I returned to Maplewood Road on my own. Mark had to go back with Mr. Ashburton. He had been asked to help Mr. and Mrs. Stoat with Paul's belongings, such as they were. I telephoned Harriet, then Tom and later Sarah. But they were all out. I felt abandoned now myself when I needed them, as in my turn, I had when they needed me, abandoned them. A time to mourn indeed.

To dispel these gloomy unconstructive thoughts I went to bed with a gin and tonic and two flakey bars. For reading matter I took a Mills and Boon novel lent to me by Liz Ely. She feels she herself could write a romantic novel, and is going to try her hand, she said. I found it most amusing, although I suspect this reaction was not envisaged by its author. On every page someone vibrated, pulsated, writhed or shook with desire and it all sounded most exhausting and improbable. Perhaps it was simply the mood I was in, feeling relief after the solemnity of the funeral, but I chuckled out loud more than once. It could be that the gin helped me to see the comic side of the romantic novel. But perhaps it was meant to be funny, I don't know for certain.

Tuesday 16th July

Today Mrs. Pratt spoke of her liaison with Terry McGough. It was a true love affair, she said, much like the one I was myself conducting with Mark. She added that she thought that she and Terry were made for each other. That they were both married to other parties seemed churlish of me to point out, but I did venture to say that both Mark and myself were single people and thus the affair she was conducting, and the affair I was conducting, bore little or no resemblance. Mrs. Pratt did not agree. "It all comes to the same thing in the end" she said. I don't know why she said this because it is not true.

Mrs. Pratt said she and Mr. Pratt were not compatible and never had been. This was not at all the impression I had had when I first went to work for her, nor do I believe it to be so. She and Mr. Pratt seemed to have a very jolly life with their mutual interests in caravanning, and modem dance competitions taking them hither and thither. Sometimes I think to justify our behaviour we recall our past to suit ourselves. I suspect Mrs. Pratt needed to convince herself, more than she needed to convince me, of her reasons for unfaithfulness. In truth, there probably were very few valid reasons. Her marriage was, no doubt, as good or bad, happy or unhappy, boring or not boring, as anyone else's. She just wanted, I suspect, what most people want in their lives, something that is mostly absent, and that is magic. I am sure Mrs. Pratt's marriage, after 29 years, lacked magic, but when out with Terry McGough magic abounded. She was for an hour or two transported into a mystical world of touch and light and laughter and who could blame her, in truth, for choosing this enticing path to the much duller one to which she was committed. "Everyone is entitled to a bit of fun, a bit of happiness," she said, "as long as it doesn't hurt anyone, I can't see any problems." But it always does hurt someone, I thought, even if the someone is only yourself. Anyway I didn't voice that feeling to Mrs. Pratt. Inevitably passion beats prudence, and the voice of reason is lost in the storm. And, for that matter, saying it I would sound like a complete prig. On the way home I bought a bottle of gin. I needed the gin to assist me to tackle a letter from the tax office. It seems so complicated I can't even understand the questions, let alone know how to answer them. Gin might help.

Saturday & Sunday, 20th & 21st July

Today, in Somerset I met Posy Trevelyan. She is a pretty girl, with long blonde hair and seems tall for her twelve years. She was exceedingly pleased to see Mark but I think considerably less pleased to see me. Mark has had no long-term woman friends since Anna left and Posy is not willing, or used, to sharing his attention when they infrequently meet. We are staying at "The Gateways" a small hotel just outside Exeter and this afternoon we walked over moors covered with sheep, and purple heather. The sun shone for us and I think, and hope, Posy was happy.

We had a dreadful dinner, such as only the English can produce without much effort, in the hotel dining room which was empty and cold, and smelt of furniture polish. Posy said that she thought her mother was enjoying her Sociology Course. But, she said, she thought she was a little lonely and hadn't made many friends in Exeter. She, Posy, for her part, quite liked her school but not as much as the school she had attended when they were all living in Yeovil. Where, incidentally, she wished they were still living. Before we went to bed, we watched a film on the television in the hotel lounge. I saw it, without seeing it, since I was thinking of something quite else. It is the children of divorced parents who suffer most, I thought. They have to witness scenes and experience traumas which they did not ask for, and do not wish to be party to. I myself inflicted this situation on Harriet, Tom and Sarah. I betrayed them as Mark and Anna betrayed Posy. We should all, all divorced parents, stand condemned. "JC" I said later in bed "forgive us our trespasses as we forgive those that trespass against us ..."

Sunday. I said untruthfully that I had a headache this morning and suggested Mark took Posy out somewhere without me. She was delighted with this idea. They went to Porlock and sat on the beach and, it seems, had a good time. On the way home Mark told me that Posy had said she hoped, every day, that he and Anna would discover that they still loved each other. And, having discovered this truth, that they would re-marry and then they could all live happily together as a family again. This is what I would like best, she had said. She did add that she didn't dislike me, but simply that she didn't want Mark to have a girlfriend, whoever she was. What she wanted was both her parents to live together in the same house as her, and to get on with their everyday lives as they used to, before the divorce. And that I suspect is what all children wish for but which sadly, with our current one in three statistics of marital breakdown, many are denied. For the rest of the journey, we were both silent.

Thursday 25th July

Father Murphy came to see me. He was over-wrought and looked ghastly. He hadn't shaved for several days and his eyes had a wild look. It needed no effort on my part to imagine the cause of his distress. In Biblical terms, Father Murphy now knew Molly O'Shea and, having known her, he was now awash with guilt and paying the inevitable price for transgressing. He needed to talk, and talk, and I let him. Not only was he bitterly disappointed and angry with himself over his inability to resist temptation, but he seemed bitterly disappointed with the act of sex itself. I got the impression that he thought it most unfair that he was suffering endless guilt as the result of an act which purported to be unique and, which in his opinion, had proved much less so. "A bit of a confidence trick, Missus," he said. Perhaps Molly O'Shea with all her flesh revealed, was far from the creature of his imagination, the reality of her less exciting than the fantasy. Poor Father Murphy should have read Proust, who maintained, I gather, that the fantasy of anyone was always more attractive than the actuality. He talked for at least two hours. Perhaps like Mrs. Pratt, to convince himself more than me that human weakness was universal and that he was, after all, only a man and made of flesh and blood like other men. And that since it only happened once nothing had, in actual fact, changed. He still believed in the vows of chastity and the Roman Catholic Church. "How could one act of sexual intercourse change one Missus" he said, "it was something so transitory, so very transitory that I could blot it out of my mind, I could forget all about it, couldn't I?" he pleaded to me, repeatedly. I reminded him of a line I read from a novel by Anita Brookner, which said "once a thing is known it cannot be unknown." But at least, I said, God will forgive you, but you may have more difficulty with His Representatives on Earth who are, it is said, less generous with their absolution. Father Murphy left me, tired out from talking, but a little more cheerful I thought. I wondered, when making scrambled eggs for supper, what would happen to Father Murphy when the High-ups in the Church of Rome learnt of his misdemeanour. Ex-communication will be his lot, I suppose, and I feel a degree of sadness for him. Because what else could he do, or be?

Sunday 28th July

The dean's text for the sermon in the Cathedral this morning was concerned with Faith and Intellect. A subject I must say I am very interested in since they have been, hitherto in my mind, contradictory. Thus, I listened intently instead of allowing my thoughts to wander off on other matters. The conclusion he had come to, it seems, was that reason and spirituality are not, as one would think, incompatible. He said religious faith can enrich a part of one's nature which would otherwise remain unfulfilled, and that he thought a belief in some spiritual purpose in our lives, seemed better than none at all. It does, in the end, come to a personal faith, he said. This assertion must be the truth since we have no real knowledge of how another person experiences faith, or in what form. We know nothing about their exact communications with God or His with them. All we do know is what they tell us, or what we see when we watch them at prayer which is, of course, an unreliable way of judging. Instead of praying they could, in fact, be thinking about the washing left out on the line, or perhaps planning how to put their mother-in-law off for next Sunday lunch. Their thoughts could stray to a mistress or lover that can only be seen on week days and wondering whether this Sunday will ever come to an end. Rodney Ely probably thinks along these lines when he is giving the appearance of a man at prayer.

 This evening Mark and I had our first ROW. It was about Faith, or the lack of it. I have avoided until now discussing Christianity with him since I knew it was a subject upon which we would disagree. It is a large area of incompatibility between us that I see no easy solution to. I knew shortly after I met him that he was not a Christian. Indeed he declares himself a conscious agnostic and believes in no God, no Higher Being whatsoever. But there is "a time to keep silent and a time to speak" and I know when Mark denied the existence of God that I had to disagree. It is of course much easier to argue the case against there being a God than arguing the case for his existence. The same questions are always asked by every disbeliever, and Mark was no exception. Why does your God allow so much suffering, so much inequality, so much sorrow and so on? And of course, since I am not omniscient, I myself have no idea why He allows these things. I wish I did. It is solely my Faith that allows me to believe in His word and in Him. That is all I have in His defense and it is pitifully inadequate against logical and scientific reason. Then frustrated perhaps by my own inarticulate protestation I sat down on the floor and wept. Mark comforted me and said it should not be an issue between us, people must be free to believe or not believe as they wish, he said. But I know it is an issue and I feel sad and scared in that knowledge. Mark left early, and I made a cup of tea, ate two Mars Bars, and went to bed to discuss important things with myself. Anna and Mark apparently had no such problems over the existence of God. For them in this at least, they were united in knowing there was no such being.

AUGUST 1985

The heat, the misery, the disorder, the humidity, the traffic jams, the holidays, the tourists, the noise, O God, I HATE August. I wish I could go to sleep on the first of August and re-awake on the first of September annually, since for myself August has nothing whatsoever to recommend it. I can't even write my diary in August; my heart just isn't in it. I shall, therefore, just write down a few moments I would like to remember in my old age, of August 1985.

Sarah and I went to Scotland to stay with Diana and Hugh Cassington-Mackenzie. We hired a small disagreeable car which had problems starting, proceeding and stopping. In it we lurched up to the West Coast where Diana and Hugh have a small holiday house. Into this house they cram a host of friends and neighbours, who shout at each other, loudly and endlessly. They talk of the sizeable fish they have caught, or the excellent stalk they have just returned from, and how many stags they shot, or how they know for a certain fact that the Pilkington-Erskin's gillie is having an affair with Lady Penelope Fortescue-Mathieson-Currie from the next glen. Conversations in Scotland, as long as I can remember, ran on these lines. How many birds killed, how many stags shot, or how many fish caught and who is enjoying who, up and down, as it were, which glen. Stories procure poor marks for the teller unless several lesser persons such as gillies, stalkers or gamekeepers are in the fray. A kind of continuous real-live version of "Lady Chatterley's Lover," takes place with (as in other amateur dramatics) different players acting the lead parts each season. I don't think there is an equivalent of this sport in England, but of course there may be in Cotswold villages or in any other small upstairs/downstairs community left in the 1980's. But it is a very beautiful part of Scotland and Sarah was asked to not a few highland flings where kilted men twirled her around the dance floor, an activity which she seemed to enjoy. Although she was approaching eighteen

Laura and Sarah became friends and went off to do things together. Diana and I, thus carefree, made ourselves delicious picnics and climbed high up onto the open moors behind the house to eat them. We found there another land, a deserted place, which I felt sure was the top of the world. Incredible views stretched indefinitely, elusively. In the heather's dark purple sprays we sat gossiping and laughing as if we were teenagers again, pupils together at St Anne's, instead of two middle-aged women. Diana, not known for her large vocabulary, said her lover was still wonderful, being in love was wonderful and making love with him was wonderful too. And although it was sheer agony, she said, not seeing him this month he, poor man, was having to suffer his own family at a seaside resort in Brittany. She had however received two letters from him, the contents of which swore undying love for her, within the constraints of a marriage which, she must understand, he couldn't ever leave. Well, goodness me, plus ça change. I spoke a little of Mark and I but somehow it all sounded dull in comparison to Diana's frenzied affair. Accounts of secret meetings, furtive telephone calls, agonizing weekends to live through when communication was impossible, and passionate if hurried sex in hotels during the afternoon when she was officially at china-mend classes, were difficult to beat. The stuff of life is drama I suppose, and relationships that lack dramatic appearance are I think to outsiders enormously insipid. Sarah told me on the journey home that she thought that Gus Ely was more interesting, well she said "cool", than the kilted ex-public-school men she had met in Scotland, but nevertheless she had enjoyed herself and even admitted that good manners were an advantage in a man. I said that good manners were an advantage and an attraction in anyone, and thought as I said it, that I sounded exactly like my own mother. Sarah simply said God what a boring observation.

Mark's parents were staying with Aunt Eliza at Farnleigh House during the last week of this intolerable month. We joined them for the August Bank Holiday. (Does a bank holiday mean a holiday for the banks, I wonder?) For my part, I think Bank Holidays should be banned altogether. The road we took to Portsmouth overflowed with cars, looking exactly like those newspaper cartoons that might amuse us when we ourselves are not participants in the picture. Talk about life imitating art. As expected, Aunt Eliza was in her element, with all of us there. Her stories grew more and more outrageous, with bandits kidnapping her in the Amazon Basin, and finding drugs planted on her person in Hong Kong, placed there by desperate heroin smugglers. On that occasion she narrowly escaped prison but for the help of the British Consul. Colonel and Mrs. Trevelyan knowing and understanding her well, encouraged these fantasies and even suggested others she might have had. I became well acquainted with the Trevelyans in those four days. We picnicked on the Hampshire Downs, visited churches, went to a Mozart concert at the Gladstone Rooms and played bridge one evening. Mrs. Trevelyan and I did a considerable amount of washing up together which is a good way of getting to know someone. She loves books and writes novels herself, and although they have never been published she doesn't seem to mind. She writes because she likes writing which seems to me the best reason for so doing. She understood Colonel Trevelyan well, I thought, allowing him to think he was the family's General-in-Chief whereas in fact she herself quietly made the decisions. The Colonel was a true gentleman in the old-fashioned sense of the word, with courtly good manners and strict principles. He desired nothing more than the proper order of things as he understood them. A definite chauvinist, but a good man according to his lights and I liked him well enough. Mark and he disagreed on most subjects discussed which disconcerted Aunt Eliza. She told them how boring it was for the rest of us when they argued. Would they kindly stop she asked. But they continued in spite of her pleas and I tried to remember what the wise have said about Fathers and Sons over the centuries - but I couldn't. Was it something to do with jealousy, I wonder?

We all embraced on leaving, and Aunt Eliza wept unashamedly. We had a lovely time at Farnleigh and were sad to leave late on Monday night. On the Winchester By Pass travelling home, Mark asked me to marry him. Then he said before I could suitably reply, we needed to stop for petrol as the car was running on an empty tank.

At home, in bed, I told him I couldn't think of anything more lovely in the world than being his wife and I would be very pleased to accept his offer. At dawn I awoke, feeling apprehensive. Why, I asked myself, and then remembered the pledge I had given Mark. For some reason, I felt depressed.

Tuesday 3rd September

The shop was deserted when I arrived today. Its interior smelt of dead flowers, and dank, poisonous water. It had been empty over the Bank Holiday and in the heat, many plants had not surprisingly died. I set about putting things to rights. Mrs. Pratt arrived after ten o'clock, looking tired and ill. Lighting a cigarette she said, "God, I hate Bank Holidays, I mean who wants bloody Bank Holidays, anyway." She glanced at the wilting flowers, stumped into the lavatory, slammed the door and stayed there for quite some time. From this outburst I deduced that life was not going well for Mrs. Pratt. Bank Holidays are traditionally bad times for married people in the throes of an affair and I suspect Mrs. Pratt had not seen, or spoken to Terry for a much longer time than she would have wished. Poor old Mr. Pratt I don't suppose his Bank Holiday had been very diverting with his wife in such a turmoil. I made Mrs. Pratt a cup of coffee, and she said, wearily, that she hadn't been in to water the plants over the Bank Holiday because she herself had been feeling unwell. I said I was sorry to hear it and hoped she would be better soon. I asked her whether she was enjoying her affair with Terry McGough, and whether things were going well. This line of questioning was not, as it turned out a good one, since Mrs. Pratt, her face puckering burst into tears and sobbed into a large red handkerchief. She muttered something, but, since she had the handkerchief over her face most of it was lost to me. I did catch words such as 'bastard', 'shit', and 'twister', which gave me to understand that Terry's behaviour had not pleased her in some way. Later, she told me that he had stood her up on Thursday night. They had arranged to meet in the Three Elms Public House, Station Road, at 7 o'clock, but although she waited until 8.30 fortifying herself with gin and limes, Terry put in no appearance, he did not arrive. She had had no word since and was worried sick she said. Her friend, Mrs. Bradley, who she went to see yesterday told Mrs. Pratt that she had seen Terry out in a car with a young woman, when she, Mrs. Bradley, was shopping in town on Wednesday. How did I interpret that, Mrs. Pratt asked me. Had I given a truthful answer I would have said briefly: the writing on the wall, very clearly written in Capital Letters, no less. But what I did say was just because Terry was seen with a young woman in his car did not mean, in particular, that he was conducting any sort of liaison with her. Perhaps it was his daughter, or a friend of his daughters I suggested. "He will probably ring you today with an explanation for his absence, and all will be well." I said in addition, because I know Mrs. Pratt appreciates this kind of sentiment: "the path of true love never runs smoothly, Mrs. Pratt, as you and I know." When I left the shop the telephone had not rung and in my estimation except for customers ordering bouquets, or somesuch, nor will it.

Saturday 7th September

Today, not without considerable difficulty, I bought a second-hand car from Westwoods Garage, Wellchester. I selected one I thought suitable for the small amount of money I have available. A slick-suited salesman seeing me, a woman alone, approached with his smile and his patter. It was lucky I had picked that particular car he said, as it only had, as it happened, a one-woman owner well-known to the garage for her virtues. For myself, I wouldn't think a garage would recognize a virtue if it was delivered in a marked box - but I digress. It had 52,000 miles on the clock but the slick-salesman said it was only three years old. "Which" magazine, I pointed out, advised that an average motorist travels between 10 and 12,000 miles a year, and this particular car appeared to have registered 22,000 miles over and above the amount expected or wished for in a three-year-old car. "True, very true," said man said, "but the bodywork is in perfect condition." I admit I know little of cars but I assume that this factor is one of the least important in their purchase. From any car I own, I have one single positive and unalterable requirement, reliability. When I get in it I require it to start, and when I apply the brakes I absolutely require it to stop. And, in between the two carry me smoothly to my destination. But, rather like love affairs, running, buying and maintaining a good working relationship with a car seems much more difficult than first imagined. I decided not to buy the car purported to have had one lady owner since the salesman seemed anxious to get rid of it, but bought instead an Escort whose owner, or owners, were not known to the garage for their virtues. I hope I haven't made a mistake. Making such a large purchase on my own is quite a worry. I think, on reflection, women should only go to garages intent on buying a car with a man to accompany them. Feminists, I am sure, would be angry hearing such a statement, but I believe it to be true. Men who sell cars, in general I would say, think of women as incompetent and ill-informed on motoring matters, and treat them as complete nincompoops. The assertive side of my nature had improved, but I am still pretty wet and next time I wish to change or buy a car, Mark, will I hope, accompany me. Incidentally, the car is white.

Sunday 8th September

The Cathedral was very empty this morning. Perhaps people were still stuck in traffic jams from the succession of Bank Holidays. Or perhaps they had suffered so much shock and stress venturing out in August's commotion, that they had decided to stay at home, and watch a church service produced by a television company. I must say I find it astonishing whenever I have watched a service on the television how the church in question, somewhere quite obscure in the Welsh hills, Devon valleys or even an inner-city church, invariably happen to be on that particular day, full to overflowing with people. I have thought to myself, without charity perhaps, that it might be something to do with the presence of the television camera catching them singing hymns, and at prayer. Rodney Ely took my collection, he was looking pious but nevertheless I thought he looked well pleased with himself.

Tom and Harriet came for lunch. Tom has been staying in Harriet's London flat for a few days, and was returning to Brighton tonight. He is going there to look for a rented house as he no longer wishes to live at home with Leo and

Grace. There is never any food in the house, he said, and Grace objects to his music. And, Grace and Cathy's alliance has ceased since Cathy used the washing machine leaving an Indian scarf in it, which went unnoticed by Grace when she next used it. Unfortunately all Grace's silk underwear designed no doubt to excite Leo, are now orange. I am sorry, I said, which was not true. We walked, traditionally, along the canal path in the afternoon, and saw the swallows flocking together in the skies, getting ready I suppose for their long journey south. I always feel overwhelmed when I think that a bird, no bigger than an outstretched hand, will have flown some 6,000 miles by the time it returns here in the spring. What strange instinct drives it to do this I wonder - certainly modern man has no similar drive. In fact, it is quite difficult to make some people move six feet, let alone 6,000 miles. Harriet told me she has a new boyfriend called George. She will bring him down to stay on Saturday 21st, she said. I already feel warm towards George as he is an accountant. Perhaps, if he wished to impress, he will help me with the incomprehensible tax forms I have accumulated, read and despaired of. I said nothing to the children about my engagement. Another time, I thought.

Tuesday 12th September

Had an hysterical telephone call from Diana Cassington-Mackenzie. Would I tell her how was she going to survive, how could she continue existing, was it possible to die from a broken heart, did people deprived one from another pine and fade away completely, until the flesh left their bones and they became as to dust, ready to be carried away by the four winds? And much more in this vein but those just quoted are representative of the general gist of the conversation. The reason for Diana's destitution was, apparently, that THE LOVER, a merchant banker it transpired, had been posted to Hong Kong for five years and was leaving England at Christmas. That this was bad luck I agreed, but that Diana's whole life would be completely amorphous, without hope or love, or even a moment of joy or pleasure in consequence, I could not concede. In fact, I said rather tersely that if I remembered correctly this was not the first of her love affairs to disintegrate, and that I thought in an astonishingly short time she had not only recovered but found a substitute. "God Almighty, Victoria," she said, "where is your compassion? Here I am desolate, needing consolation, support and understanding, and you are about as much use as a dead cat." She went on to say that I had changed since leaving Leo, everyone said so, and nobody thought it was an improvement on the Victoria they used to know. As I write this in bed I thought about Diana's accusations. Was I less kind, less anxious to please, less interested in the flotsam of life, than I had been? Was I now a touch self-righteous and proud when before my divorce I thought less than nothing of myself, scarcely indeed existed outside the wife/mother role? As a married woman of my generation I had not been required to think, merely to be. My verdict and conclusion, as my own judge and jury is that I have changed. I am now more selfish and more assertive and my needs are, I think, important. Therefore probably I am less attentive than I was in the role of friend, or mother, but I am happier with myself and more self-confident. Thus I would say that it was a change for the better, not for the worst.

Wednesday 18th September

I was 43 today. I received seven birthday cards which was very cheering. Nothing from Tom but Harriet and Sarah remembered. Liz, Rodney and Gus sent me a card, although I suspect neither Rodney or Gus knew that they had done so, since Liz signed the card for them. Father had managed a card with this message printed inside in silver letters:
Thinking of you Dear
On your Birthday
Loving Thoughts, Mother and Father
He had crossed out the "Mother" bit with a biro. I assume this card was procured for him by Mrs. Hill. It was not previously known to me that father had Loving Thoughts at all, least of all about me but it is nice to know I am wrong. The other three were from Diana, Mrs. Pratt and Mark. I placed the one from Mark, depicting a Renoir type lady in a sea of flowers on my bedside table, and the rest I put on the mantlepiece in the sitting-room. I thought I would weep all day as I had one on my 40th, 41st and 42nd birthdays but no such thing occurred, I shed no tears. I was felicity itself in the shop, even smiling politely at a harridan woman customer who was being particularly difficult and demanding. Mrs. Pratt presented me with a gift-wrapped box of lavender toilet soap and powder from Boots. I was

touched. It was kind of her especially considering she was herself being plagued by her nerves due to Terry's still unexplained silence. "Don't worry, Mrs. Pratt, there is time yet" I said to her. "Not that much time dear," she replied, "my time is running out." I thought this rather witty on her part, but it was my birthday and I felt magnanimous, allowing perhaps my judgement of wit to fall below its usual standard.

Tonight Mark took me out to dinner at the Crown Hotel. The very place where we had met and fallen-in-love on a spring afternoon, earlier this year. The dining-room which I hadn't seen before, was wood-panelled. On each table there were small parchment shaded lights, and single roses in small white china vases. We had a stupendous dinner and drank a bottle of champagne. I became quite merry and Mark had to restrain me from singing an old army song I know, not in the least suitable for the dining-room of the Crown Hotel. As a matter of fact, I think it might have cheered a few of the other diners up. From what I could tell most of them looked on the miserable side, and were not, it seemed, having a good evening out at all.

At home, in Maplewood Road, Mark gave me his present. It was a beautiful engagement ring fashioned out of an aquamarine, with small seed pearls surrounding the stone. He slipped it on my finger, and said "I love you, Victoria." I kissed his cheek, thanked him and said "I love you too." And I felt, I am sure, as delirious as all those ladies do in Mills and Boon romances, when the hero on the ultimate page, declares his love. And why not?

Saturday 21st September

This afternoon as Harriet and George were coming to stay I made a red cabbage and pork stew, and an apple tart. Dusting about I listened to "Any Questions" and wondered as I do every Saturday why the B.B.C. ask such ridiculous people onto the panel. With intolerable, opinionated M.P.'s from either side, shrill feminists, and somebody KNOWN, all talking at the same time, they sound like angry rabble not articulate and wise which is, in my opinion, how they should.

Harriet and George arrived at about six o'clock. He seems most congenial, clever, and, I would judge, kind. And, for someone from a Good Public School the usual dose of arrogance seems to be missing - so what is the Achilles heel? There must be something but it is, as yet, hidden. Harriet seems very happy and we had a jolly evening. Mark was on duty this weekend, so it was just the three of us. Gone are the days of passage creeping, I thought, as I heard Harriet and George enter the spare room together and firmly shut the door. It is I know less hypocritical behaviour, but surely it is less "fun" too, having permission, as it were?

Sunday 22nd September

Harriet and George said that they would like to accompany me to the Cathedral. It was, of course, lovely being there with them. The Cathedral itself looked magnificent with shafts of sunlight peeping through the stained-glass windows, settling themselves on the massive stone pillars which support the Centre Aisle. The saints all appeared quite content, pleased perhaps that the tourist season was nearly over and that less people now stared at them every day and took their pictures; a situation which they had every reason to dislike. The sermon was about not laying treasures up for ourselves on earth where moths and rust might corrupt them, or where thieves could break through and steal which reminded me that I broke the catch in the kitchen window last week. During the sermon I noticed that Harriet and George were holding hands. The sight of the two hands joined together, in my Cathedral, made me feel envious and jealous in a way that quite astonished me. Preparing lunch I poured myself a very stiff gin and tonic to steady my nerves which seemed to be racing about in a positively uncontrolled way.

    Harriet and George left at teatime. I sat in front of the fire and read David Cecil's delightful biography of Jane Austen. She lived by four principles, he said. These were good sense, good humour, prudence and good manners. I wish I could say the same for myself, particularly the good sense.

Wednesday 29th September

    Father Murphy came to tea. There were no traces left of the red dye he used on his hair, or his beard. They were now quite white. He looked much older. "I'm a broken man, Missus" he said "or I will be for sure." Next Wednesday, on

October 2nd, he has an appointment in the town of Gloucester to see the Bishop of Eames, a man known for invincibility and harsh measures both in the church and with his priests and flock. For his confession, Father Murphy had asked to see someone outside Blackfriars and this morning he had heard that he was to see the Bishop of Eames. Father Murphy was still angry with himself, "God knows what possessed me, Missus, to make such a foolish move - I can't understand how God let me lapse in that way," he said. "I thought you knew Father Murphy" I said, "that God gave you Free Will and this being the case your behaviour is entirely your own responsibility." He then asked me whether I had ever been a school mistress, or a person in authority over others and I said I had not. "What a pity" he said, "You would have been tip-top at that job." I concluded that he thinks I am bossy and boring, school mistresses in general giving this impression, although speaking for myself I know several who are no such thing. One indeed I know, has occasional sex with a builder from Bath. A bit of rough, she calls it, which compliments her lifestyle.

    I suggested to Father Murphy that we had an early drink which he agreed was a great idea. I put on my tape of the Dubliners and we joined in with the singing of Finnigan's Wake, McAlpine's Fusilier's and Seven Drunken Nights, and after two or three drinks each, we did some Irish country dancing. Father Murphy was quite a dab hand at dancing, a fact I had not previously known. To excuse myself for this disgraceful performance I am persuaded that it was cathartic for Father Murphy to dance and sing on the way, as it were, to collect his death warrant and final condemnation.

Wednesday 2nd October

Lunch at the Poppy's Tea Rooms with Liz. I was very pleased to see her. Liz is so sensible and constant. I know precisely, beforehand, what topics we will discuss and just what her opinions will be, opinions formed early in her life and which have not changed one jot since. I find this most soothing; a reliable unchangeable friend is essential for sanity and wellbeing. Everyone should have a Liz Ely. In fact before I met her I felt Jill Archer was a friend in that category although of course since she lives in Ambridge, (the Archer's Radio Programme) the friendship was forced to be somewhat one-sided. Liz said Gus was going to India after Christmas, travelling about, as people do. I myself can never visualize what it is that travelling people do and how they manage. I mean where do they do their teeth, or buy Beecham's capsules against colds, or wash their underclothes, or any other clothes that need attention. A spirit of adventure is imperative in order to traipse about the world with a knap-sack, a spirit which in my own make-up is entirely missing. Travelling into Wellchester on the 83 bus is bad enough. In September Liz had joined a Writers Group, and she was enjoying it very much, everyone was friendly and supportive, she said. It took place on Tuesday nights and she had told Rodney and Gus that she would therefore not cook their dinner on that night. They could manage themselves, she said. This had come as something of a blow to Rodney and Gus, they had always thought of Liz as caring for their needs before her own. She told them that they were mistaken in this assumption. Since reading articles available in the library, she was learning to be more assertive. She told them apparently that in future if and when she wanted to attend a course, see a film, or spend Saturday afternoon in bed with a book, that was what she was going to do. Since this outburst Rodney, she said, who had been, over the summer, out at many more weekend conferences and business evenings than ever before, had quite changed his tune. Last week he asked her whether she would like to go to a film with him, or even dine out, a previously unknown suggestion. It was, I think, Margaret Drabble who once said: "marriage was a safe harbour from which to have excursions," but I think that when the safe harbour is perhaps no longer as safe as it was, the excursions are less frequent and less fun. Could this supposition apply to Rodney I wonder? I would guess it could.

Friday afternoon, Saturday & Sunday, 4th, 5th & 6th October

Mark and I went to stay at a farmhouse this weekend in the Suffolk' marshes. The roads east to west or west to east in England are almost unassailable and it took us nearly as long to get from Wellchester to Brent Cudley, as it would have taken us to get from London Airport to Moscow. But it was worth the effort when we arrived in the spectacular county, where the east wind blows in sharply from Siberia. The pink, green and yellow houses with interwoven oak beams came as such a surprise to me, they are so singular, unprecedented anywhere else in England that I know of. Lavender Hill Farm House was large and comfortable, and our bedroom, white walled with sloping beamed ceiling, looked out over a slow running river which flowed through the garden and wound into the fens. On Saturday we visited the Guildhall in Lavenham, and in the evening we dined in a restaurant well-known for its gourmet menu, and rightly so. The magic Mrs. Pratt had longed for, and looked for was certainly in evidence for us this weekend. Everything was perfect, never have I felt happier and in harmony with a man. Never had I loved Mark so much, or he me, I think. Holding hands in silence on Southwold beach on Sunday morning, we stood and watched a ship on the skyline, until it sailed out of sight. And then we walked far on the deserted beach, to the sound of seagulls' screams and the slapping sea. And it was magic time. But after lunch, the return drive to Wellchester seemed never ending, and a certain melancholia overcame my spirits for no reason that I knew.

Tuesday 8th October

Matron rang early this morning to say that father was unwell. Nothing serious, but she thought he would like to see me. I went this afternoon. He seemed more depressed than ill, but he did have a cough on his chest for which he was taking a linctus. He complained a little about his teeth saying they had never afforded him any pleasure since I had taken them to the dentist earlier this year. I decided on listening to him talking that his depression was due to the fact that Mr. Fentley had died suddenly in the night, last week. Of course, Father could not endure Mr. Fentley but it had been diverting annoying him, having a sparring partner, as it were. I think now, ather felt a large void in his life with no-one to fight and nothing much to plan in the way of disturbance. Father hasn't talked about mother since her funeral but today he said, in a tone of anger, that she shouldn't have died and left him on his own. He implied that she should have waited to die until such time as he gave her permission. "But she was always headstrong" he said. God, some people are insufferable. My mother was the epitome of crushed womanhood. But she never grumbled, never thought father was the bullying, preposterous chauvinist pig that he is, or if she did she never showed it. Headstrong, mother headstrong, how dare father even think it, let alone say it. I left him, promising to bring some more whisky next week, the thought of which perked him up considerably. I expect by then he will have found a new enemy to pester and plague, which will shake off his doldrums in no time.

Monday 14th October

Mark telephoned with dreadful and frightening news. Posy, bicycling back from school had been knocked down by a lorry and had sustained head injuries. Very little detail did he know except that she was now in the Exeter Hospital Intensive Care Unit. He had just spoken to Anna and was going down to Exeter tonight to stay with her. Together they would go to see Posy tomorrow. Mr. Ashburton had given him leave of absence until Friday, or more, depending on Posy's condition. Mark sounded grim, his voice shaking with shock and apprehension. I asked whether I should come over to school to comfort and help him but time was short and I think he wanted to be alone. He had to pack and arrange for other members of staff to stand in for him while he was away. "I will think of you darling, and pray for Posy" I said, as he rang off. I did pray for Posy tonight. "JC" I said "please make something good come out of this accident so that your Will is not completely incomprehensible, even to those with FAITH." I took four homeopathic pills purporting to be sleep inducing before I turned out the light. These were not successful in my case and it wasn't until dawn that I fell asleep.

Wednesday 15th October

Mark telephoned. He said that Posy had multiple head injuries and was unconscious on a ventilating machine. The doctor said she could have a brain clot but this would not be known until she had a CT scan later in the week. And, if she did have a clot she would need an operation. The doctor has expectations of a recovery, but says that at this stage it is difficult to predict what will happen precisely. She could be in the Intensive Care Unit for several weeks, and then would need constant care and attention, Mark said. But if things are unchanged tomorrow he will come back to Wellchester on Friday.

I put on Beethoven's Fifth Symphony and sat in the arm chair by the fire and wept.

Friday 18th October

Mark telephoned. He is back in Wellchester. There is no change in Posy's condition and a neurosurgeon is seeing her on Monday. Anna has moved into the hospital, staying there night and day. Obviously when Posy recovers consciousness one of her parents or both must be beside her. For Mark, at the moment, this is impossible. Mark is on duty this weekend and I cannot see him. I feel estranged and desolate.

Sunday 20th October

I went to Matins in the Cathedral this morning, but it did nothing to uplift my spirits. We sang three of the gloomiest hymns I have ever known and, even if the sermon had been spectacular in its content, from where I was sitting I couldn't hear more than one word in ten, so its eloquence was missed by me at least. Looking down the empty pew I thought enviously of Harriet and George sitting together, holding hands, when we came here three Sundays ago. Childishly, I thought life is not metered out in equal portions at all; that it is indeed, unfair.

Sarah was at the house when I got home, a friend from Marlborough had dropped her, she said. I had nothing much to cook but we made a rice hash from tinned minced meat and carrots which was, if not delicious, quite edible. Sarah announced as we walked along the towpath this afternoon that she did not wish to continue her A level studies at Plato College. And, that she did not like the girls there, nor did she like Marlborough - the most boring town in the world, she said, and she hated chemistry, physics and math's which were the subjects she was supposed to be studying. "I was happy in Brighton" she said, "when you and Dad were married, nothing for me has been so good since then."

    This evening I drove Sarah back to Marlborough and told her when I dropped her that I would think about her request to leave Plato College, and see what alternatives there might be to suit her better. She hugged me, but ran in through the College gates without a goodbye or a backward glance.

Tuesday 22nd October

    Father Murphy came to tea. HE HAD BEEN REPRIEVED. I put the tea back in the cupboard and ran down to Crabtree's Off License and bought a bottle of champagne. The Bishop of Eames was most understanding, said Father Murphy, when he confessed his sins. He has, of course, to be punished but the punishment is that he is to be sent back to Ireland, to an enclosed monastery. But Father Murphy thought this quite tolerable compared to being excommunicated. He is leaving before Christmas, and is looking forward to it. "The reason I think I got off lightly, Missus" said Father Murphy, "is that with all the controversy about homosexuals making up a quarter of all priests, and the complex problems of ordaining women, a single sinful act of heterosexual weakness is not enough to fuss about unduly, I should say." "I wouldn't know," I said, "Church Statesmen move in mysterious ways, like Christ, it seems." We opened the champagne and toasted each other laughing and crying and generally behaving as if Father Murphy had been released from the Tower of London, escaping execution. It was, I suppose, the last party I would have with Father Murphy, and I wanted it to be memorable, and it was. "God bless you, Missus," said Father Murphy, passing out on the sofa some hours later. I remember going up to bed, but what time it was I do not know. When I got up, Father Murphy had gone.

Friday 25th October

"All men are bastards" was Mrs. Pratt's text for this morning. Mrs. Bradley had told Mrs. Pratt what her friend, Mrs. Robinson, had told her. Mrs. Robinson, whose daughter Linda worked part-time in the Three Elms Public House Lounge bar, said that Terry McGough and a very common piece of work had been drinking in there on Saturday night. And no-one, said Linda, could construe their behaviour as that of just good friends. In actual fact, she reported, they were all over each other in quite a disgusting way. Mrs. Pratt had herself not unexpectedly heard no word from Terry. In her bitterness Mrs. Pratt had now taken against the Royal Family. She seems to think that they are to blame for her affair and its demise, and holds them directly responsible for her unhappiness. If, she said, they set a better example, as they should, ordinary folk would follow suit and the country wouldn't be in its present disgraceful immoral state. "The Young Royals have morals of alley cats," she shouted at me. "Just look at them, screwing all over the place, regardless. No wonder things are out of order." I said very little, but it was all that was required. Mrs. Pratt was vexed beyond endurance and simply wished to pour out her distress uninterrupted. She will not in future, she said, be going to the Caravan Touring Club meetings since the class of person to be met there is no longer to her liking.

Monday 28th October

Mark had two free periods this afternoon and we met at Cathy's tearoom in Mereton Ogmore. He has telephoned every day since the accident and I knew Posy had had an operation to remove the blood clot last week, and that she had started to improve as a result. On Saturday Anna had seen her hand move. I had not seen Mark since our weekend in Brent Cudley, and the change in his appearance was striking. He had lost weight and lines had appeared on his hitherto unmarked face. Anna, he said had had to abandon her Sociology Course in order to virtually live at the hospital, and Mark wished to share some of the burden. Obviously journeying from Wellchester to Exeter, even on his free weekends, was difficult and expensive. He was thinking of other possibilities, he said, should Posy have a lengthy stay in hospital. Mark said Anna was behaving admirably not fussing and keeping cheerful and optimistic. He was going to stay with her next weekend, and take his turn by Posy's bedside.

I felt a variety of overwhelming emotions while Mark was talking; love, jealousy, anger, resentment and compassion all jumbled up like a box of coloured ribbons. But I was silent and simply held his hand, tightly, under the white cotton table cloth. The Escort performed well on the way home which was fortunate since I couldn't see clearly, my tears distorted the view.

Thursday 7th November

Diana Cassington-Mackenzie came for tea, and stayed the night. The Lover, she said, was off to Hong Kong next month and she felt much dispirited. She had forgiven me for speaking to her sharply when she telephoned with the bad news. "You are a bit stuffy and opinionated, you know Victoria" she said, "but I suppose since your life is untroubled, you can afford to be wise." "Nothing is ever what it seems," I said, "and that statement could not be further from the truth." I told her about Mark, Anna and Posy and the confusing emotional problems I was experiencing. Diana was very sympathetic and was, I felt, pleased that I was beset by difficulties too. The bonds of friendship are strengthened it seems through each other's misfortunes, and not, oddly, through each other's felicities. I suggested to Diana that she started an Open University course, which might be ideal for her energetic and active brain to tackle, the pursuit of knowledge instead of the pursuit of men. Diana was quite taken with the idea, and said she would think about it. We made, or in fact I made, scrambled eggs for supper and we opened a passable bottle of white wine, most of which Diana drank rendering her incapable of driving home. In these circumstances she stayed the night. I did enjoy our evening but I do wish she wouldn't chain smoke Marlborough cigarettes. The house smells like a Public Bar.

Sunday 9th November

The much-loved words from Corinthians, chapter 13, read at this morning's 2nd lesson helped me make the monumental decision I had been debating since I agreed to marry Mark. "For now we see through a glass darkly, but then face to face; now I know in part, but then shall I know as I am known." For my part, although I cannot see clearly, I can see sufficiently to know that I cannot marry Mark. I know that I could not live with someone whose fundamental beliefs were completely contrary to my own. I know that however much I love Mark, however much I enjoy our literary discussions, our dances in the kitchen, and making love, and however much magic pervades our meetings making them seen other-worldly, without him being able to share, or at least understand my love of God, uniting ourselves in marriage would be intolerable, and destructive to us both. It is too big a disparity between us. As I walked home, I felt a curious relief. Had I not recently observed to Father Murphy that we know in ourselves what is right, and, this being so, that we can do no more than follow our consciences.

Monday 11th November

Unaware of Mark's timetable since Posy's accident I telephoned him tonight to arrange a meeting, as soon as possible. The decision I had made to break off the engagement must, I felt, be told to him immediately. I wished to give myself no time to procrastinate or change my mind. When I got through to him I asked about Posy. He said her condition was still unaltered, although she had moved her hand again, and that he spoke to Anna on the telephone every day. I asked him to dinner here on Saturday night, and he said he would come. "I love you and miss you darling," he said as he rang off, "and I look forward to seeing you on Saturday, so much." I shouted out loud into the empty sitting-room "Oh damn, damn. Mark why did you have to say that, tonight," and I poured myself a soothing, silvering gin-and-tonic, searching for my pocket handkerchief the while.

Friday 15th November

    Mrs. Pratt told me she was selling Rose's Flower Shop, and moving up to Derby to be near her daughter, Lyn, and grand-daughter, Karen. She thought she would make a new start, and find new friends and interests. She and Mr. Pratt could see more of their grandchild, she said, and acquaint themselves with any others born much better in close proximity. Estate Agents are coming today to value the shop and she will sell it and her house, as soon as she can. I said this was an excellent idea and thought that she would be much happier in Derbyshire, which is the truth. In actual fact I had never thought Mrs. Pratt's heart was in Rose's Flower Shop. She had little aptitude for either selling flowers or arranging them. She liked neither the customers nor the flowers, and hearing her profanities when calculating her books makes me that that bookwork was not something she found pleasure in either. And for myself, how did I take the news? I was pleased. Nine months in a flower shop was all I wanted of flower shop experience, and can only hope that whatever I have learnt, will come in useful somewhere. Perhaps, for instance, if Harriet marries George, I will be able to arrange the wedding flowers. I said to Mrs. Pratt that I would stay until the middle of December, and we decided that despite its associations, Friday December 13th would be the appropriate day to terminate my employment.

    Mrs. Pratt said that she and Mr. Pratt were going to have a drink in the Black Bear Public House, Mereton Ogmore, this evening. "Mrs. Pratt" I said, "Douse yourself in perfume, dress yourself up, put on your high heels and observe Mr. Pratt. See if you can detect a look of desire in his eyes. It could be that you have been looking for magic in the wrong place. Perhaps it was in your own home, Mrs. Pratt, but you didn't see it because you were not looking in the right place." Mrs. Pratt lit a cigarette. "Well, you could be right, dear," she said, "I might just give it a whirl, see if there is life in the old dog yet." And we both laughed. Magic, I thought, as I walked home, invariably needs a conjuror to help it happen.

Monday 18th November

Liz and I had lunch together in Mark's and Spencer's. When it is important Liz is a good listener, and she sat quietly, not interrupting, as I told her of my decision not to marry Mark, why I had made it and how upset I was. In fact, Liz is a regular churchgoer herself, although I have always thought her devotion was more apportioned to the social life it brought her than a spiritual affinity with God. But who knows? She said she understood my reason for the choice I had made and, although she thought she would not have made it herself, she would support me in it, absolutely. In addition I told her about Mrs. Pratt going to Derby and that I would, in consequence, be leaving my job in the Flower Shop in the middle of December. Liz then said that a Mr. Timms was retiring at Christmas from her job in the library, and that I should apply for the vacancy when it came up in the New Year. She would put in a good word for me, she said. It could suit me well as I need a full-time job and what nicer employment than to work amongst books, like Philip Larkin. I wonder what qualifications are needed. I have heard that in these times of fierce competition that except possibly for the position of lavatory attendant, or road sweeper, 2 A levels are almost universally required for any job at all. If this is the case with the library vacancy, with no A levels, and only 2 O levels, one in cookery, I wouldn't ever get an interview, but I will await optimistically until after Christmas. I could invent some foreign qualifications, I suppose, and perhaps I will.

Saturday 23rd November

I woke at dawn with a leaden heart. Mark was coming to dinner and I was to tell him of my decision. This was my first thought, and the continuing one throughout the day. I made a very special dinner, his favourite mushroom soup followed by ox-tail and mashed potatoes. I bought some French brie and two bottles of wine. When Mark arrived my heart was thumping, and I felt faint and weak at the knees. Not only, I think, because I was to break the news but seeing him in the flesh and loving him as I do I hoped I would not lose my resolve. I asked him how he was getting on with Anna. "Better," he said smiling, "than I ever did when I was married to her. And of course, since Posy is our child, in this respect, we feel close to each other." He said that he and Anna decided yesterday that he should give in his notice to Wellchester School. He wanted to work and live nearer to Posy than he did at the moment. He, himself, resolved to tell me that news tonight. He was not thinking of a broken engagement but simply that he would be living somewhere near Exeter for an indeterminate time, and perhaps would have, one day, an invalid daughter. I told him at this moment that I couldn't marry him. "I have thought about this from the beginning of our relationship and tried to believe that it didn't matter," I said. "But I know now that the difference we feel about the existence or non-existence of God means that I could not be happy living with you, as your wife. I love you dearly, darling Mark" I said, "in fact more than I have ever loved before and it is not an easy choice I have made. Moreover, I believe that you should have another try living with, and loving Anna, so that when Posy recovers she will receive the best present of her life, her constant wish come true, as it were. You and Anna together, loving each other and loving her, as a family should."

Mark simply said he felt very tired. He wanted to go home and think. It was all such a shock, he said, and he needed time to reflect by himself. He left, kissing me gently on the cheek, and I sat by the fire long after the wood burned to ashes, and wept at my great loss.

Sunday 24th November

I could not go to the Cathedral this morning. If Jesus Christ is to be my partner hitherto, He will have to acclimatize Himself to my moods like anyone else would. In fact I stayed in bed all day spoiling myself with treats. I made a tuna fish sandwich for breakfast with fresh coffee and orange juice and carried it upstairs to eat on a tray. I read passages from "Emma" that make me laugh, particularly ones containing garrulous Miss Bates - dear me, she talks more than any living woman I know; except those heard on "Any Questions." In addition, I read passages from a Jackie Collins novel left here by Tom. This informed me about matters that I had not previously ever envisaged or guessed at, but interesting nevertheless. I consumed two Mars Bars, and smoked the stub of a Gauloise cigarette I found in the ashtray, and, I drank a quantity of gin. By early evening I felt distinctly ill and tried to focus my mind on people less fortunate than myself. However, I couldn't think of anyone.

Thursday 28th November

An old Steve McQueen film was on at the Gaumont and this evening I went to see it. Perhaps, I thought, watching Steve striding about, being in turn provocative, wicked, and seductive, screen lovers are the best lovers. They never disappoint us, they are consistent, and age does not weary them. There are no losers when involving yourself with a screen hero, your heart is guaranteed not to break and in this particular love affair, you are quite safe. It never does.

Wednesday 4th December

Father Murphy who is sailing for Ireland next week came to say goodbye. He was looking sprucer than I had seen him for months, much less wild and haunted and he had regained the lost weight. His hair and his beard were once again a hennaed red colour and the silver cross that lay on his chest was restored to its former sparkle. We sat a little primly in the sitting-room sipping our tea from the bone china cups of my best tea service, and talked of commonplace things. An outsider would not have guessed what emotions, traumas and stresses had taken place in Father Murphy's life this year, or in mine. He appeared now a confident and happy man. Life, I thought, ebbs and flows, crises are fought and won or fought and lost and life continues, regardless. "I am certainly looking forward to going, Missus," he said, "it will be great to be back in Ireland." "Well, look after yourself, Father Murphy, keep a clear head and your hands in your pockets" I said, smiling, as we embraced at the door. I don't know why I said that about keeping his hands in his pockets. I must have thought, at the time, that it was good advice. I watched him walk jauntily down Maplewood Road until he turned the corner, and was out of sight. I went back to the sitting-room and poured myself a drink. I shall miss him more probably, than I wish to think about.

Wednesday 6th December

    I received a letter from Mark. He has been given compassionate leave and has gone to Exeter a week before the end of term. He is currently staying with Anna. They were taking it in turns to stay with Posy who has blinked her eyes a little this week which made them excited about her recovery. The last paragraph of the letter was about us. Mark said he found the real danger of Posy's condition made everything else in his life seem less urgent, if not less important. It was difficult, he wrote, to be in love with a woman and then, in a moment, exchange her for another, even if the other was his ex-wife. It was all so bizarre and confusing. Look after yourself, darling Victoria, he wrote, I miss your jokes and funny face more than you know. The decision you made in not wishing to be my wife and the reason you gave for it, is no doubt, the right one, and I admire you for the courage taken to make it. Nevertheless, I love you.

I tuned into the Archers in time to hear Peggy wingeing on about something she was unable to purchase in Martha's shop. I wish there was a vacancy in Martha's shop I could apply for; it always sounds so cosy there, so solid, ordinary and uncomplicated, quite unlike life's realities, as I know them.

Monday 9th December

I went to see Father at Blueberry Rise this afternoon. He is still in a gloomy mood. He complained about his teeth, Mrs. Hills' familiarity and slapdash nursing, the domestic's staff dusting the room inefficiently and the low standard of television films. That was some of the complaints but not the whole list. Suddenly sitting by his bedside I absolutely knew I had to ask him to stay with me for Christmas. Now I had a car I could fetch him on Christmas Eve, with no real problems. "Would you like to stay with me for Christmas this year, Father," I heard myself say. "Stay with you at Christmas, Victoria" he said, "Of course, I would like to stay with you. It was bloody horrible staying here last year. Dangerous pieces in the pudding as one hazard to contend with and there were plenty more. Staying with you would surely be an improvement on that." I didn't rise but simply told him I would arrange with Matron to fetch him on Christmas Eve and that there would be a good supply of whisky for him to drink at Maplewood Road. "Good," he said, and appeared much less dispirited than he had when I arrived. It is said I think that virtue is its own reward. I sincerely hope this statement is correct although I doubt it in this instance.

Friday 13th December

Rose's Flower Shop has been bought by a Fast Food Company, Mrs. Pratt told me, on my last morning in her employment. Someone had made her an offer last week, she had accepted, and completion will take place soon after Christmas. I had today bought a bottle of white wine which we drank in our break instead of coffee. Mrs. Pratt was happier now the decision was made to leave Wellchester, and she said she was looking forward to going to Derby. "Quite some members of the Royal Family live in Gloucestershire." she said, "and I am hoping to see them in the flesh when Mr. Pratt and I take day trips to the Cotswold countryside." "But Mrs. Pratt, I protested, "I thought the Royal Family were quite out of favour with their libertine behaviour and general dissipation." "Well you know dear" she said - Mrs. Pratt has just started calling me dear lately - "I have always taken a keen interest in the lives of the Royals, it's a habit of a lifetime and difficult to break. My own life is now somewhat dull, with nothing much of interest to add a sparkle to it, but discussing the Royal Family, almost as if they are my own relations gives me great pleasure, and adds a little glamour to my life." I said I could understand this sentiment and vowed silently to myself that I would never laugh at people again whose life was enhanced by Royal gossip. We drank the wine and became loquacious. Mrs. Pratt confided to me that she hoped Terry McGough would contract Aids and, if I ever heard that he had, would I please send her a post card informing her of the good news. Although it is most unlikely, I said I would, should I hear. I didn't tell her about the broken engagement between Mark and myself, the mood was not conducive. "Take care dear, and all the best," she said waving farewell as I left.

Tonight I tried reading Proust again, and found no improvement in its content or in my interest. As I turned out the light, I thought of how fond one gets of the oddest people - people like Mrs. Pratt for instance.

Tuesday 17th December

Diana came to lunch. She was looking very attractive. Short skirts suit her and the bright red one she sported was certainly short. It barely covered her knickers but, if I had legs like hers, I too would wear short skirts. Like the Walrus and the Carpenter we talked of many things, ambition, loneliness, lovers, stiff joints, the menopause and its symptoms, and what we hoped for in the future. And we talked of our children and whether we had failed them, and if we had, did they forgive us for failing. We came to no clear conclusions, and nothing exceptional was said but talking is comforting, and we comforted each other in our various needs. Diana has applied for The Open University course, and I decided I might do likewise. It ought not to be beyond my capabilities to study academic work in middle-age, even with the brain cell deterioration I keep reading about. And, something interesting to look forward to in 1986.

Diana gave me a tin of Assorted Herbal Teas from Harrods. An early Christmas present for which I was, of course, most grateful.

Friday 20th December

Sarah arrived at teatime today and said she had decided to stay with me for Christmas this year. Her luggage was a profusion of plastic bags which now seem to be everywhere. Query: why doesn't anyone under 25 own or use a suitcase? Why when travelling anywhere do they take their belongings about in plastic bags. I cannot understand it at all. Perhaps it is not 'cool' to carry a suitcase, in the same way that it is not 'cool' to wear a raincoat. My children, I know, would certainly prefer to get pneumonia than protect themselves, coat-wise, in a downpour. And telling them that arthritis will be their lot in years to come, from their own negligence, is considered one of my most boring observations and not worth the slightest attention.

We went for a drink tonight in Hertford Road, with Liz, Rodney and Gus. The house was draped festively with silver tinsel, and pieces of holly with red berries were angled over the pictures. Trust Liz, I thought, to find holly with berries. I never can. The only holly that I ever bought at Christmas time looked like leftovers from last year, limp and grey and sprouting absolutely no berries whatsoever. Another couple arrived who I had seen in the Cathedral, a Mr. and Mrs. Sutcliffe. Mr. Sutcliffe was very tall, thin and pale, and he talked unceasingly. Mrs. Sutcliffe, on the other hand, was small, plump and silent. In fact, that is not quite true because at one point in the evening she said her sister Dolly from Manchester, would be joining Mr. Sutcliffe and herself at Christmas. Sarah had left the sitting-room for somewhere else, and I, representing middle-age, had to continue drinking Bristol Cream Dry Sherry for another unremitting hour. When Sarah and I eventually, and most happily I thought drove home Sarah told me Gus was going to India after Christmas. She would like to go too she said, and was going to ask Leo to pay her fare. When I was married to Leo it was difficult enough to get him to pay my fare to London, on a journey he wished me make, so I should think Sarah's chances of a ticket to India are minimal. But who knows?

Later we watched "Gone with the Wind" on the television. I said I thought Scarlet O'Hara was magnificent but Sarah did not share my opinion. She said she thought Scarlet O'Hara was crap.

Saturday 21st December

At lunchtime when Sarah was shopping in Wellchester, Mark telephoned. I still feel weak when I hear his voice, and still tremble when I hold the telephone. Well, I love him, I suppose. Posy, he said, had briefly opened her eyes yesterday and the doctor predicted improvement daily from now on. He and Anna were so excited and encouraged by this, they had gone out to dinner together, as the doctor suggested they could do with a break. "We are going to try living together again as man and wife" he said, "and not only for Posy's sake. We think, and hope, that perhaps we have learnt good and helpful things about each other during this crisis, and about ourselves during the time we had on our own. We hope this knowledge will help to make a second chance together, a definite possibility. And, if it works Posy will have the love and security she so desires." "Oh good, Mark" I whispered, "I do hope it all works for you. All my best wishes and, of course, all my love." As I put down the receiver I thought about The Sermon on the Mount where Christ gave out a list of some of the noblest of human ideals. Feeling noble was an experience I was not enjoying myself at that moment. In truth, I didn't want to be blessed for being a peace-maker or for hungering after righteousness, knowing that I would be rewarded in heaven; no, indeed, I wanted Mark for myself, to love me, and for me in my turn to love him. But only for a moment. Mark's place was with Anna and Posy, his family no less. And in reality, I knew this to be so. When Sarah came home she didn't guess about the tears because I had put on a mask of make-up. I told her that it had come through the letter-box, as an advertising gimmick, and I was taking advantage of it since it was free. She believed me, or, if she didn't, she didn't say so.

Sunday 22nd December

Apart from myself and a sprinkling of others, the Cathedral was empty this morning. Perhaps even regular churchgoers feel that attending church twice in a week is a surfeit of worship, and, since they will have to go on Wednesday, absenting themselves today was quite legitimate. God no doubt would understand this argument. For my part I am extremely glad I went since the sermon was taken from my favourite text, Ecclesiastes 3. "To everything there is a season, and a time to every purpose under the heaven." And all those other times listed in this chapter were read out too:

> A time to be born, a time to die, a time to plant, a time to pluck up that which is planted, a time to kill, a time to heal, a time to break down, and a time to build up.

> A time to weep, a time to laugh, a time to mourn, and a time to dance, a time to cast away stones and to gather stones, a time to embrace and a time to refrain from embracing.

> A time to get and a time to lose, a time to keep and a time to cast away. A time to rend, a time to sew, a time to keep silence and a time to speak.

> And a time to love and a time to hate. A time of war and a time of peace.

I have copied this out now from my own Bible, because it is simply so beautiful, and as near the truth as we can get, I suppose. After the service I sat down for a while and I thought about how my time had been spent in 1985. It had passed in a moment, certainly. I had myself laughed, and wept, and danced, sewed, embraced and refrained from embracing. And I had kept silent and I had spoken at the appropriate time, hadn't I? In a single year much had happened, much had been learnt. I wonder whether I will be able to put it to good effect, next year? I hope I am a little wiser but the learning process, has I thought, to be a continuous one. But, if there is indeed a time to every purpose under the heaven, then this year of 1985 was my time, and purpose, I believe to learn about loving. About receiving love and giving it away. Until this year I had not known about love as I do now; its passions and its demands, its great joys and its great agonies. I had witnessed for myself, and for my friends and for my children, different aspects of this phenomena called love. But, for my part, I realized that the love of God outweighs all other loves and that its denial would be impossible for me to contemplate. Before I left the Cathedral I made a wish. I wished that Posy would recover soon and completely from her accident, and that she would get the united and happy family she deserves and hopes for. In effect, I wish for Poppy a time to build up, and a time, to dance.

Tuesday 24th December

A little before lunch Sarah and I went to fetch Father from Blueberry Rise. He is, I think, worried about staying here and I know I am worried that I shall not manage to care for him. as he expects to be cared for. But Sarah is here and Harriet and George are coming for lunch tomorrow. No doubt they will all help me. Quite a family party we will be this year, I thought, as I put my Christmas cards on the mantlepiece. I saw a message on the back of the card from Guy Bell, overlooked when I first read it. It said: Have been in America for six months, and am just back in time for Christmas. Will be in Wellchester on January 7th, would you like to meet me in the Wellchester Arms at 7 o'clock? Don't bother to answer, just come if you can. Well, Guy Bell, I might, I cannot say what I shall do next year, yet.

As I got into bed tonight exhausted, I opened Philip Larkin's book of poems. Inevitably it opened on the page of the poem that I have read the most: "they fuck you up your mum and dad, they may not mean to but they do." And I thought Yes, Philip Larkin, they do, they do, again, and again and again.

Suddenly I felt hungry, and thought to myself that abstinence on the eve of a Great Festival was hardly in order. I opened therefore a bottle of white wine, (Sancerre) ate a Mars Bar, and waited for Christmas and the New Year. Sitting in the old armchair I thought of Mark. Will he remarry Anna in the New Year, and make Posy happy, I wonder, or are things in reality, not as easy as that? I suspect they are not, but as Mrs. Pratt might have said - only time will tell. And I have time, I have time.

Acknowledgements

I would like to thank Tiffany Watson and Jessica Deguara, my daughters, for their constant support of my blog and my poems.

Thank to Francis Harrison, my partner, for his support in all things.

Many thanks to Peter Moran who, once again, comes to my rescue and pieces this book together for me. I would be lost without him.

By the same author:

Poems from Grace Cottage - 2006

More Poems from Grace Cottage - 2009

A Collection of Poems - 2016

The Ragbag of a Human Heart - 2019

Realisation - 2020

acotswoldpoet.blogspot.com
where you can read my weekly blog.

Printed in Great Britain
by Amazon